Lady Macbeth of Mtsensk

Lady Macbeth of Mtsensk
A Sketch

Nikolai Leskov

Translated by Robert Chandler

ET REMOTISSIMA PROPE

100 PAGES

100 PAGES

Published by Hesperus Press Limited

4 Rickett Street, London SW6 1RU

www.hesperuspress.com

First published in Russian in 1865

This translation first published by Hesperus Press Limited, 2003

Introduction and English language translation © Robert Chandler, 2003

Foreword © Gilbert Adair, 2003

Designed and typeset by Fraser Muggeridge

Printed in the United Arab Emirates by Oriental Press

ISBN: 1-84391-068-3

CONTENTS

Let me begin with a whimsical hypothesis. Imagine, if you will, that some mad cultural commissar has decreed a moratorium on all forms of literary creation and publication for, say, the next fifty years. Who would suffer? A legion of frustrated writers, naturally, whether real or self-styled. A legion of hardly less frustrated book reviewers. And, yes, all those readers for whom a novel is 'relevant' only if it is set in the present day (and I do mean 'day', not 'year' or 'decade'). But who else? Given that the past millennium has accumulated a backlist of neglected classics so lengthy it would keep even the most insatiable reader occupied for a lifetime, I would suggest absolutely no one.

One of these neglected classics is *Lady Macbeth of Mtsensk*. In fact, Nikolai Leskov's novella is a work whose title, at least outside of its country of origin, tends to ring a more resonant bell than the name of its author. The Shakespearean reference helps, of course. In addition, for many of us the bell rung by the title is less that of Leskov's 1865 original than of Shostakovich's 1934 operatic version (which, in the wake of a damning article in *Pravda*, the composer subsequently revised and renamed *Katerina Izmailova*); and even, for a handful of cinephiles, of Andrzej Wajda's 1962 film adaptation, retitled in English *Fury Is a Woman*. About Leskov, then, it would be fair to say that, although he was a model and a master to his compatriots, admired by Gorki and Chekhov, his international reputation has failed to keep pace with that of his single most celebrated work.

But what of the work itself? *Fury Is a Woman* sounds like nothing so much as a lurid pulpy thriller, and perhaps the most remarkable quality of *Lady Macbeth of Mtsensk* is how uncannily it anticipates the twentieth-century (and primarily American) genre of noir fiction. Confronted with the indefatigably scheming Katerina, we find ourselves thinking not of the heroines of Tolstoy and Turgenev but of those single-minded, double-crossing dames, as hard as the nails they so obsessively file and polish, who haunt the novels of Raymond Chandler and James M. Cain.

Yet that is not how she has always been 'read'. Shostakovich, for example, was widely credited with having 'humanised' her, with having rationalised and mitigated her serial killings as an anti-bourgeois act of rebellion by embedding them in a precise social, historical, ideological and, not least, pre-Soviet context. Of Katerina, *his* Katerina, the composer claimed that she 'is a young, beautiful, intelligent woman stifling in a world of vulgar tradesmen. She is ensnared in a joyless marriage. The murders she commits are not true crimes but a revolt against her milieu, that disgustingly sordid milieu in which the mercantile class lived in the nineteenth century.' He sought, in short, to transform her into a Madame Bovary of Mtsensk.

Opera librettists have historically taken quite outrageous liberties with even the most prestigious literary texts, and Shostakovich's interpretation is a lot more legitimate than most: Leskov's heroine can indeed be inscribed within a long novelistic tradition of young (or youngish) married women belatedly awakened from the torpor of loneliness and lovelessness by a devouring sexual passion. But what now strikes us most forcibly about Katerina is the terrifying absence of psychology, in place of which the novella offers only a kind of demented logic. Walter Benjamin once wrote that 'Mystical exaltation is not Leskov's forte. Though he occasionally liked to indulge in the miraculous, even in piousness he prefers to stick with a sturdy nature. He sees the prototype in the man who finds his way about the world without getting too deeply involved with it'; and the impact which *Lady Macbeth of Mtsensk* makes on the contemporary reader is all the more powerful and troubling for the abdication, unusual in nineteenth-century fiction, of even so much as a hint of authorial judgement. Never deigning to moralise or editorialise, never once intervening to express his own approval or disapproval of his protagonist's behaviour, the laconic Leskov confines himself merely to *reporting* (he was, not incidentally, a journalist by profession) the atrocities committed by the monstrous but all too human Katerina.

Most curious of all, however, is that the novella, regarded as something of a shocker in 1865, continues to shock even now; and, as the horrors it describes have been overtaken many, many times since, in fiction, the theatre and especially the cinema, it might be worth asking why. I would propose the following: that there is an innately a-historical dimension to artistic scandal and controversy.

Consider *No Orchids for Miss Blandish*, a little-known British film adaptation of James Hadley Chase's notoriously sadistic thick-ear thriller. In its own day – 1948 – it was deemed the unsurpassable apogee of screen violence and was actually banned for many years. Watched today, it's a joke, except that, since a modern spectator cannot help reinstating it within its historical context, even as he watches it, it is still, obscurely, a queasy-making experience – maybe for no better reason than that the victim of its (now relatively tame) violence is not, say, Steve Buscemi but Sidney James.

So with *Lady Macbeth of Mtsensk*. In view of the routine amorality of so much current fiction, its graphic violence and ferocious sexual candour, one could be excused for expecting the shock value of Leskov's novella to have been immeasurably diminished by the passage of time. That this happens not to be the case is a consequence not merely of its author's own storytelling gifts (Benjamin's essay on him was titled, precisely, 'The Storyteller') but also of the frisson that such a work continues to provoke when we read it a century and a half after it was written and project ourselves, as we instinctively do, back to the less tolerant and more strait-laced period of its original publication.

– Gilbert Adair, 2003

INTRODUCTION

No great Russian writer of the nineteenth century is so little known to the English-speaking reader today as Nikolai Leskov. This is in part because of the remarkable variety of his novels, stories and journalism; literary historians tend to prefer writers who are easier to pigeonhole. It is also because of the complexity of his language. To Leskov, according to one critic, 'language was not simply a medium of communication, but a potential art object in its own right, something to be played with, sculpted into interesting shapes'.[1] The language of *Lady Macbeth of Mtsensk*, though simpler than that of some of Leskov's work, moves between the colloquial, the folk-poetic and the pseudo-educated; these shifts of register are not easy to translate. The more transparent language favoured by Tolstoy, Turgenev and many other Russian realists demands less of a translator.

Even in Russia Leskov has been persistently undervalued, under both the Tsarist and the Soviet regimes. During his lifetime he was more popular with the public than with the critics. Religious conservatives disliked him for his undoctrinaire liberalism, while the radical socialists who dominated the literary world disapproved of his religious concerns. Leskov has also suffered from the misfortune of being identified with his characters, many of whom are bigoted and xenophobic. This is especially absurd: while having a deeper understanding of provincial Russian life than any of his contemporaries, Leskov was also extremely open to Western ideas. He was strongly influenced, for example, by British low-church morality – perhaps because

1. Hugh McLean, 'Nikolai Leskov', in *Encyclopedia of Literary Translation into English*, ed. Olive Classe (London/Chicago: Fitzroy Dearborn, 2000).

one of his aunts was married to an Englishman (or possibly a Scot; there is some confusion about this, compounded by the fact that the name of his aunt's husband was Scott).

Leskov's ancestry was unusually hybrid. His maternal grandfather was an impoverished gentleman who married a merchant's daughter. His father, though technically ennobled as a result of promotion in government service, came from a line of village priests; dismissed from his administrative post after a conflict with the provincial governor, he retired to the country to farm a small estate. There Nikolai Leskov grew up in close contact with the peasantry, and much of his education – although he did attend the Oryol Gymnasium for several years – was informal. All this combined to endow him with a broader knowledge of Russian society than any other writer of his time. Leskov himself wrote that, since he had grown up among the common people, it was not for him 'either to place the peasants on a pedestal or to trample them beneath (his) feet'.[2] Aged sixteen, Leskov began to work for the civil service in Oryol, moving to Kiev two years later. This was followed by three years of work in estate management, for his uncle's firm Scott & Wilkins; a position which entailed a vast amount of travel, over the whole of European Russia.

It was in 1860 that Leskov began his career as a professional writer, living briefly in Moscow and then in St Petersburg. His first major works were *The Musk Ox* (1863), a first-person narrative in the voice of an eccentric radical, *Life of a Peasant Woman* (1863) and *Lady Macbeth of Mtsensk* (1865). Two of Leskov's greatest works, *The Sealed Angel* and *The Enchanted Wanderer*, both published in 1873, explore Russian spirituality; the former is one of the few adequate portrayals in

2. Hugh McLean, *Nikolai Leskov: The Man and His Art* (Cambridge, Mass., London: Harvard University Press, 1977), p. 115.

Russian literature of the life of the Old Believers, the outlawed schismatics who rejected the seventeenth-century liturgical reforms and who, by the end of the nineteenth century, made up a fifth of the country's population. The most famous of his short stories, 'Lefty' (1881), is about a Russian blacksmith who, using nails invisible to the naked eye, contrives to shoe a dancing steel flea that had been made for the Tsar by some English blacksmiths. The nails, unfortunately, weigh the flea down; it is no longer able to dance. The story's brilliant language, dense with malapropisms and wordplay, provides an entertaining commentary on Anglo-Russian cultural differences and misunderstandings.

Lady Macbeth of Mtsensk is Shakespearean in both its linguistic vigour and its emotional intensity. Leskov was not the first writer to transport a figure from Shakespeare to the Russian provinces – Turgenev had already published his story 'Hamlet of the Shchigry District' – but none of Leskov's contemporaries, not even Dostoevsky, ever came so close to recreating the essence of Shakespearean tragedy. While writing this story, Leskov appears to have frightened even himself. According to a friend, he once said, 'while I was writing my "Lady Macbeth", the effect of overstrained nerves and isolation almost drove me to delirium. At times the horror became unbearable; my hair stood on end; I froze at the tiniest sound I myself had made by a movement of my foot or by turning my head. Those were painful moments, and I shall never forget them.'[3]

Like *Macbeth* itself, Leskov's story is closely knit. The plot is simply and effectively propelled by means of a sequence of physical embraces and grapplings. Sergei, a young womaniser,

3. Maclean, p. 151.

first embraces Katerina Lvovna, the wife of his employer, as they play at wrestling; that same evening, by then in her bedroom, 'Sergei lifted his mistress into the air like a child and carried her into a dark corner.' These two sexual embraces soon lead to Katerina's murderous embrace of her husband: '*In a single movement* she pushed Sergei out of the way, jumped at Zinovy Borisovich from behind, and, before he could reach the window, grabbed him by the throat with her slender fingers and threw him to the ground like a sheaf of newly cut hemp.' A subsequent murder, this time of a small child – '*in one movement*, (she) covered the poor child's face with a large down pillow and threw herself on top, her firm resilient bosom pressing against the pillow' – leads to the work's tragic denouement. As Katerina Lvovna and Sergei cross the Volga on their way to penal servitude in Siberia, Katerina twice flings herself on the younger woman for whom Sergei has abandoned her: 'she seized Sonetka by the legs and, *in a single movement*, leapt overboard, taking Sonetka with her... just then Katerina Lvovna appeared from another wave, rose almost waist-high above the water and flung herself at Sonetka like a powerful pike attacking a roach. Neither of them was seen again.'

In a single trajectory the work moves from the initial portrayal of Katerina Lvovna's life of overwhelming boredom (*skuka*) to her final transformation into a pike (*shchuka*). Moved either by exalted love or by the basest of animal instincts, Katerina seems to know nothing of the contradictions and hesitations that are central to our humanity; everything she does, she does 'in a single movement'. The importance of the theme of animal instinct is further emphasised by the parallels and contrasts Leskov repeatedly draws between the behaviour of his protagonists and that of a variety of animals: an imaginary pig, both real and imaginary cats, real dogs, a horse, a mouse, a nightingale, a quail and crickets – as well as the pike and roach of the final paragraph.

The story's simplicity of movement and archetypal intensity may well account for Dmitri Shostakovich's decision to choose it as the basis for his opera. David McDuff, one of the story's previous translators, has commented on the degree to which 'the narrative means, almost operatic in their simplicity and dramatic intensity… are entirely merged with the stormy, passionate nature of the heroine'.[4]

Shostakovich and his librettist introduce changes to the plot, but the story's emotional world is recreated faithfully. Shakespeare, Leskov and Shostakovich all evoke what could be described as a totalitarian state of the psyche: the heroines of all three works subordinate every thought and feeling to a single drive. This sets in motion a process of evil whose momentum is unstoppable. As Shakespeare wrote in *Troilus and Cressida*:

> *Then everything includes itself in power,*
> *Power into will, will into appetite;*
> *And appetite, a universal wolf,*
> *So doubly seconded with will and power,*
> *Must make perforce a universal prey,*
> *And last eat up himself.*

On 26th January 1936 Stalin famously walked out of the Moscow production of Shostakovich's opera, which until then had been highly praised. On 28th January the article 'Muddle instead of Music' was published in *Pravda*, initiating a vicious

4. Nikolai Leskov, *Lady Macbeth of Mtsensk* (London: Penguin, 1987), pp.17–18.

campaign against Shostakovich and other artists. It is usually believed that Stalin disliked the opera because of its abrasive, dissonant modernism. It is possible that he was shocked by the opera's blatant sexuality. It is tempting, however, to wonder whether he may not have been alarmed most of all by Leskov's, and Shostakovich's, evocation of the heroine's paranoid single-mindedness.

– Robert Chandler, 2003

Note on the Text:

This translation is based on the edition in Nikolai Leskov, *Collected Works, Vol. i* (Moscow: Sobranie sochinenii, 1956). Many translators avoid looking at the work of their predecessors; others clearly do look at previous translations but feel ashamed to admit this. I find this surprising: in most fields of human endeavour, ignorance of previous work in a given field is considered unacceptable. I have been saved from misunderstandings, or helped towards a more satisfactory rendering, by several previous translators of this story: A.E. Chamot, George Hanna, David Magarshack and David McDuff. Chamot's is the least satisfactory translation, but I am grateful to him for his apt 'Live in a crowd – you walk about with many', which I have lifted verbatim. I am also grateful to my wife, Elizabeth, to whom I have twice read the entire translation out loud and with whom I have discussed many passages at great length; to Musya Dmitrovskaya, who has patiently answered countless questions about the original; to Natasha Perova, who has checked the entire translation against the original; and to Lucy Chandler, Olive Classe, Elena Kolesnikova, Hugh McLean, Mark Miller, Olga Meerson, Allegra Mostyn-Owen and Faith Wigzell.

Lady Macbeth of Mtsensk

It's only the first song that makes you blush.
Russian saying

1

Now and again in these parts you come across people so remarkable that, no matter how much time has passed since you met them, it is impossible to recall them without your heart trembling. One such person was Katerina Lvovna Izmailova, a merchant's wife who was once the centre of a drama so terrible that our local gentry, taking their cue from someone's light-hearted quip, took to calling her 'Lady Macbeth of Mtsensk'.

Katerina Lvovna was not exactly a beauty, but there was something pleasing about her nevertheless. She was only in her twenty-fourth year; she was short but shapely, with a neck that could have been sculpted from marble; she had graceful shoulders and a firm bosom; her nose was straight and fine, her eyes black and lively, and she had a high white forehead and black, almost blue-black hair. Herself from Tuskar in the province of Kursk, she had been given in marriage to a local merchant by the name of Izmailov; she did not, however, love him or feel any attraction towards him – it was simply that he had asked for her hand and she, being poor, could not afford to be choosy. The Izmailov family was of no small importance in our town: they traded in white flour, rented a large mill in the district, and owned profitable orchards on the outskirts of town as well as a fine town house. In short, they were well-to-do. Moreover, they were not a large family: there was only the father-in-law, Boris Timofeyevich Izmailov, a man of nearly eighty who had long been a widower; Katerina Lvovna's husband, Zinovy Borisovich, who was a little over fifty; and Katerina Lvovna herself. That was all. Although Katerina Lvovna and Zinovy Borisovich had been married for five years, they still had no children. Nor did Zinovy Borisovich have any children by his first wife, with whom he had lived for twenty years before being widowed. When he married Katerina Lvovna, he had hoped that God, at least through this second marriage, would grant him a son to inherit his wealth and continue the family name, but he had been no more fortunate with Katerina Lvovna than with his first wife.

This childlessness was a cause of much grief to Zinovy Borisovich, and not only to Zinovy Borisovich but also to old Boris Timofeyevich, and it was even a great sadness to Katerina Lvovna herself. First, there was the boredom of life in a barred and bolted merchant's house with a high fence and unchained watchdogs running about the yard, an unrelieved boredom that more than once reduced the young woman to a state of depression bordering on stupor; how glad she would have been, God knows how glad, to have a little child to fuss over! And second, there were the never-ending reproaches: 'Why did you have to foist yourself on a man? A barren woman should remain a spinster!' – as though she really were guilty of some crime against her husband, her father-in-law, and the whole of their honourable merchant family.

For all its ease and affluence, Katerina Lvovna's life in her father-in-law's house was a deeply tedious life. She seldom visited anyone – and even if she did go out with her husband to call on his fellow merchants, this brought her little joy. They were all so severe: they would watch how she sat down, how she walked, how she stood. Katerina Lvovna, however, was fiery and exuberant by nature, and, having grown up in poverty, had been accustomed to simplicity and freedom: running down with her buckets to the river and bathing in her shift by the pier, or throwing sunflower seed husks over the gate and onto the head of some handsome young fellow who happened to be passing just then. Now, things were different.

Her husband and father-in-law would rise at the crack of dawn, have tea at six in the morning – then off they would go to attend to their business, leaving her to wander from room to room. Everywhere was clean, everywhere was quiet and empty, lamps glimmered before the icons, but nowhere in the house was there a living sound or a human voice.

Katerina Lvovna would walk about the empty rooms, start to yawn from boredom and climb the stairs to the conjugal bedroom, which was in a high-ceilinged attic. There she would sit for a while, gazing out at the barns, where hemp was being weighed or flour being poured into sacks; she would start yawning again and be glad to doze off for an hour or two – but she would wake to that same Russian boredom, the boredom of a merchant house, a boredom so profound that, as people say, it makes even the thought of hanging yourself seem like fun. And Katerina Lvovna had no love of reading; in any case, apart from the *Lives of the Holy Fathers*, there were no books in the house.

Yes, it was a boring life that Katerina Lvovna had been living in her father-in-law's prosperous house, for five long years with a husband who showed her little affection; but, as often happens, no one was in the least concerned by this boredom of hers.

2

One spring, during the sixth year of Katerina Lvovna's marriage, the dam at the Izmailovs' watermill burst. As ill chance would have it, this happened when there was a great deal of work on at the mill, and the breach was a major one: the water dropped as low as the lowest beam, and no one seemed able to do anything about it. Zinovy Borisovich rounded up workers from the entire district and didn't absent himself from the mill for a single moment; his father looked after their affairs in the town, while Katerina Lvovna languished at home day after day on her own. At first she was more bored than ever, but then she began to like it: she felt freer. She had never been especially fond of Zinovy Borisovich and, with him out of the way, there was at any rate one less person telling her what to do.

One day Katerina Lvovna was sitting by the window up in her attic, yawning and yawning and thinking of nothing in particular until, in the end, she began to feel ashamed of doing so much yawning. After all, it was a lovely day, warm, bright and cheerful – and, through the green wooden trellis, she could see all the different birds fluttering from bough to bough of the fruit trees.

'What am I doing sitting here and yawning my head off?' Katerina Lvovna said to herself. 'Why don't I just go for a little walk in the yard? Or I could go into the orchard?'

Katerina Lvovna threw on an old damask jacket and went out into the yard.

It was sunny outside and she wanted to breathe in great lungfuls of air; and she could hear gales of laughter coming from the gallery outside the barn.

'What's making you all so happy?' Katerina Lvovna asked her father-in-law's stewards.

'We've been weighing a live sow, Katerina Lvovna,' one of them replied.

'What sow?'

'A sow called Aksinya, ma'am, one as gave birth to a son called Vasily and forgot to invite us along to the christening,' said a young man with a bold, cheerful voice. His insolent and handsome face was framed by dark stubble and curls as black as pitch.

Just then, out of the pan hanging from the crossbeam of the weighing scales, appeared the plump rosy face of Aksinya the cook.

'You devils, you slippery devils!' she cursed, trying to seize hold of the iron beam and climb out of the swaying pan.

'She weighs twenty stone before dinner and if she eats another basket of hay there won't be weights enough to weigh her with,' said the handsome young man. Turning the pan over, he tipped the cook out onto a pile of sacks in the corner.

Cursing merrily, the woman began to tidy herself up.

'All right – and how much do *I* weigh?' said Katerina Lvovna. Grabbing hold of the ropes, she jumped up onto the pan.

'Nine and a half stone,' said handsome young Sergei, after throwing some weights into the other pan. 'A marvel!'

'What's to marvel at?'

'That you weigh even nine and a half stone, Katerina Lvovna. The way I see it, a woman like you should be carried about in a man's arms the whole livelong day. You'd never tire a man out – no, he'd feel nothing but sheer delight.'

'Think I'm made of air, do you? I say I'd tire you all right,' replied Katerina Lvovna. No longer being accustomed to this kind of talk, she blushed a little; at the same time she felt a sudden longing to let her hair down, to swap saucy jokes and have a good laugh.

'You wouldn't, by God! I could carry you all the way to Arabia the Blessed,' said Sergei.

'You've got it wrong, young man,' said a peasant who'd been sacking up flour. 'What's weight got to do with it? Who cares what a body weighs? What we weigh, young man, means nothing. It's our strength, it's the strength in us, it's our strength that counts.'

'I was ever so strong as a girl,' said Katerina Lvovna, again unable to hold herself back. 'Stronger than a good many men.'

'Give us your hand then,' said the handsome young man, 'and we'll see if you're telling the truth.'

Katerina Lvovna felt embarrassed, but she held out her hand.

'Ouch! Let go my ring – you're hurting me!' cried Katerina Lvovna, as Sergei gripped her hand. With her free hand, she gave him a shove in the chest.

The young man let go of his mistress and, from the force of her push, staggered back nearly two yards.

'Some woman!' said an astonished peasant.

'Let me try a wrestling hold,' said Sergei.

'All right then,' said Katerina Lvovna. In high spirits now, she raised her elbows.

Sergei embraced the young mistress and pressed her firm bosom against his red shirt. All Katerina Lvovna could do was wriggle her shoulders. Sergei lifted her off the ground, held her in his arms, squeezed her and put her gently down on the upturned weighing pan.

Katerina Lvovna had been unable to show off any of her vaunted strength. Red and flushed, she sat on the pan, straightened her jacket, which had slipped off her shoulders, and quietly left the barn, while Sergei gave a vigorous cough and shouted out, 'Right, you numbskulls and blockheads! Fill up the sacks – and no slacking! And if there's flour left over, you'll be living in clover!'

It was as if what had happened had made not the least impression on him.

'That Sergei's a devil for the lasses!' said Aksinya the cook, as she plodded along behind Katerina Lvovna. 'The bastard's tall and handsome, he does as he pleases. Any woman he fancies he sweet-talks and flatters until she gives in. And he's fickle, as fickle as they come!'

'By the way, Aksinya, er...' said the young mistress, still walking in front of Aksinya. 'That baby boy of yours – is he still alive?'

'Of course, ma'am, and why wouldn't he be? It's them as aren't wanted as prove the sturdiest.'

'And where did he come from?'

'How would I know? Live in a crowd – you walk about with many.'

'And has that young fellow been here for long?'

'Who? You mean Sergei?'

'Yes.'

'It'll be about a month now, ma'am. He used to work for the Kopchonovs, but the master threw him out.' Aksinya lowered her voice and added, 'I've heard there was love between him and the mistress. A thousand curses on his soul – but he's a bold one all right.'

3

A warm milky twilight hung over the town. Zinovy Borisovich has still not returned from the dam. Nor was Katerina Lvovna's father-in-law at home; he had gone to the nameday celebration of an old friend, saying he wouldn't be back until after dinner. Having nothing better to do, Katerina Lvovna dined early, went up to her attic, and opened the window; leaning against the frame, she began shelling sunflower seeds. The servants ate in the kitchen, then went off to find somewhere to sleep – by the sheds, in the barns, or in tall fragrant haylofts. The last to go out was Sergei. He strolled about the yard, let the dogs off their chains, whistled a bit, and, passing beneath Katerina Lvovna's window, looked up at her and gave a deep bow.

'Greetings!' Katerina Lvovna said softly from her attic, and the yard was as silent as a desert.

'Ma'am!' came a voice, two minutes later, from outside Katerina Lvovna's locked door.

'Who's there?' Katerina Lvovna asked fearfully.

'Please don't be frightened. It's me, Sergei.'

'What is it, Sergei, what do you want?'

'Just a quick word with you, Katerina Lvovna. There's a small favour I'd like to ask of you, it's nothing important. May I come in for a moment?'

Katerina Lvovna turned the key and let Sergei in.

'What is it?' she asked, returning to the window.

'I wanted to ask, Katerina Lvovna, if you happen to have a book I could borrow. I'm bored.'

'I don't have any books, Sergei. I'm not one for reading.'

'I'm so bored,' Sergei repeated.

'But why?'

'Heavens above – how could I not be bored? I'm young – and life here is like life in a monastery. I look ahead and see nothing but a life of loneliness till my dying day. There are times I despair.'

'Why don't you marry?'

'That's easier said than done. Who could I marry? I'm a nobody – what girl from a well-to-do family would marry someone like me? And as for the poorer girls – well, Katerina Lvovna, as you know yourself, they're lacking in culture. What understanding of love can they ever have? There's little enough of that, as you know only too well, even among the wealthier folk. Take your own self, if you don't mind my saying so – to any man who has feelings you'd bring nothing but joy, but here you are, cooped up in a cage like a canary.'

'Yes, I'm bored,' Katerina Lvovna couldn't help but say.

'How could you not be bored, ma'am, living the life you lead? Even if you did, as it were, have an admirer, the way most women do, when would you ever get a chance to see him?'

'No, you – you shouldn't say things like that. If I could only have a little baby, then I think I'd be happy.'

'But ma'am, if you don't mind my saying so, a baby doesn't just come out of nowhere. I've lived long enough, you know, among merchants – do you think I haven't seen what life's like for their wives? You know the song: "If you have no sweetheart, *toskà* fills your heart" – and this melancholy, let me tell you, Katerina Lvovna, lies so heavy on this heart of mine that I'd gladly take out my steel knife and cut out my poor heart and throw it down by your little feet. Yes, I'd feel better that way, a hundred times better…'

Sergei's voice had begun to tremble.

'What are you telling me all this about your heart for? What's it got to do with me? Go away.'

'No, ma'am, please,' said Sergei, quivering all over as he took a step towards Katerina Lvovna. 'I know it, I can see it, I can even feel and understand very well that your lot in this life is no easier than mine. Only now,' he went on, without drawing breath, 'now, at this very moment, everything lies in your hands, everything lies in your power.'

'What do you – why did you come here? I'll throw myself out of the window,' cried Katerina Lvovna. Overwhelmed by ineffable terror, she clutched with one hand at the window-sill.

'My matchless sweetheart, why would you want to do that?'

Sergei whispered nonchalantly, and, pulling his young mistress away from the window, he held her tight.

'Oh, oh, let go of me,' Katerina Lvovna moaned softly, weakening under Sergei's passionate kisses and, in spite of herself, pressing closer still to his powerful body.

Sergei lifted his mistress into the air like a child and carried her into a dark corner.

Silence set in, broken only by regular ticking from a pocket watch, hanging above the bed, which belonged to Katerina Lvovna's husband; but that changed nothing.

'Go now,' said Katerina Lvovna half an hour later. Not looking at Sergei, she was rearranging her dishevelled hair in front of a small mirror.

'Why would I want to do that?' Sergei answered happily.

'My father-in-law will lock the doors.'

'Oh my sweetheart, what kind of men have you known that they can't find their way to a woman except through a door? For me, whether I'm coming or going, there are doors wherever I look,' replied the young man, pointing to the wooden posts supporting the gallery.

4

Another week went by without Zinovy Borisovich coming home, and his wife and Sergei spent every night together, until break of day.

Much wine from the old man's cellar was drunk during these nights in Zinovy Borisovich's bedroom; many sweetmeats were eaten, many kisses were planted on sugary lips, and much was the fondling of black curls on soft pillows. But no road runs smoothly for ever; all have their potholes and ruts.

One night Boris Timofeyevich was unable to sleep; he was wandering about the silent house in his calico nightshirt, going first to one window, then to another, when all of a sudden what should he see – sliding down the post beneath his daughter-in-law's window – but the red shirt of young Sergei! Astounded, he leapt out and seized the young man by the legs. Sergei swung his arm back, meaning to land a hearty blow on his master's ear, but then he stopped, realising this would mean trouble.

'What on earth…' said Boris Timofeyevich. 'What the hell have you been doing?'

'What I've been doing, Boris Timofeyevich, what I've been doing, good sir, is what I'm doing no longer.'

'Have you just been with my daughter-in-law?'

'I know very well, master, where I've just been, and I advise you, Boris Timofeyevich, to listen to me and mark my words: what's done can't be undone, and it's best not to bring shame on one's own house. What do you want of me? What satisfaction do you require?'

'I want, you viper, to give you five hundred strokes of the lash,' said Boris Timofeyevich.

'I'm the culprit, you're the judge. Tell me where I'm to go – and do as you wish. Drink the blood from my veins.'

Boris Timofeyevich led Sergei down to his stone storeroom and lashed him with a whip until the strength gave out in his arm. Sergei didn't even let out a groan, though he chewed through half of his shirtsleeve.

Boris Timofeyevich left Sergei in the storeroom, intending him to stay there until his flayed back, soon to be covered by an iron-hard black crust, had healed. He left him an earthenware water jug, locked the door with a big padlock and sent for his son.

But a seventy-mile journey on Russian country roads takes

a good while even today, and Katerina Lvovna soon felt she couldn't live another hour without her Sergei. Released into the full breadth of her expansive nature, all restraint swept away; she grew so determined that there was no stopping her. She found out where Sergei was locked up, spoke to him through the iron door and rushed off to look for the keys. 'Let him out,' she said to her father-in-law.

The old man turned purple. Never had he expected such impudence from a daughter-in-law who, however she had sinned, had at least always done what he told her.

'You – how dare you!' And he began cursing Katerina Lvovna for all he was worth.

'Let him out,' she said. 'I swear to you in all conscience that he and I have done nothing wrong.'

'Nothing wrong!' he said, through gritted teeth. 'And what was it you and Sergei got up to at nights? Plumping up your husband's pillows?'

But she just kept on and on: he must, he must let Sergei go.

'Very well then,' Boris Timofeyevich finally pronounced. 'If that's what you want, O honest wife, then that's what you'll get. As soon as your husband's come back, we'll take you to the stables and flog you with our own hands. And I'll have that Sergei packed off to jail tomorrow.'

So Boris Timofeyevich decided; his decision, however, was never to be put into effect.

5

Before going to bed, Boris Timofeyevich had some buckwheat kasha with mushrooms, and soon afterwards he began to suffer from heartburn. All of a sudden he was having spasms in the pit of his stomach; he vomited terribly, and towards morning he died, dying exactly the same death as the rats in his barns, for whom Katerina Lvovna used with her very own hands to prepare a special dish containing a toxic white powder that had been entrusted to her for safekeeping.

Katerina Lvovna let her Sergei out of the stone storeroom and, not caring two jots what others might think, laid him in her husband's bed to recover from his flogging. Her father-in-law, Boris Timofeyevich, was given a Christian burial, and no one suspected a thing. What, after all, was there to wonder at? Boris Timofeyevich had died, and what of it? He had died from eating mushrooms – like many others before him. Boris Timofeyevich was buried in a hurry. They didn't even wait for Zinovy Borisovich to come back: it was warm just then, and the messenger sent to the mill had been unable to find him there. Zinovy Borisovich had happened to hear of some timber, another seventy miles away, that was being sold off cheap; he'd gone to inspect it and hadn't told anyone where he was going.

After the funeral, Katerina Lvovna denied herself nothing. She'd never been timid, but what had got into her now was beyond belief: she strutted about, ordered people around, and never let Sergei leave her side. Everyone was full of wonderment, but Katerina Lvovna was open-handed and generous – and the wonderment ceased. 'Sergei and the mistress,' they said, 'are enjoying a little romanticness – that's all. It's her business, and it's her that'll be held to account.'

In the meantime Sergei recovered, stood tall again – and once more he was Katerina Lvovna's handsome young falcon. Once more life grew sweet. But not for them alone was time passing; after a long absence, Zinovy Borisovich, the wronged husband, was hurrying home.

6

The afternoon was scorching hot, and the flies were quick and lively and a terrible nuisance. Katerina Lvovna closed the bedroom shutters, hung a woollen shawl over them and lay down beside Sergei on the high merchant's bed. There she both slept and didn't sleep; the heat was unbearable, her face streamed with sweat, and her breathing was hot and laboured. She felt it must be time to wake up, time to go and have tea in the garden, but she had to struggle to rouse herself. In the end, the cook came and knocked at the door. 'The samovar under the apple tree's going cold,' she said. Katerina Lvovna managed to wake up and found herself stroking a cat. The cat was pushing itself between her and Sergei, a splendid grey tomcat, as big as they come… and with whiskers like a country tax collector. Katerina Lvovna ran her fingers through his fluffy fur and he pressed up against her, pushed his blunt little face into her springy breasts and all the time went on singing his quiet little song, as if he were telling a tale of love. 'How did this giant of a cat get in here?' wondered Katerina Lvovna. 'And the cream's still on the window-sill. The rascal's going to gobble it all up – I must chase him out.' She tried to seize hold of the cat and throw him out, but he slipped through her fingers like a breath of mist. 'Where on earth's this cat come from?' Katerina Lvovna asked herself in her nightmare. 'No cat's ever got in here before – and just look at the size of this one!' She tried to seize hold of the cat again – and once again the cat wasn't there. 'What's happening? Once and for all, is this a cat or isn't it?' thought Katerina Lvovna. Panic gripped her, jolting her awake and driving her nightmare away. Katerina Lvovna looked round her bedroom – there was no cat at all, only her handsome Sergei, his powerful arm pressing her breasts to his hot face.

Katerina Lvovna sat up in bed, kissed Sergei and kissed him again, caressed and fondled him, smoothed the rumpled bedclothes, and went out into the orchard to have tea; the sun had set, and a magical evening was dropping down over the baked earth.

'I overslept,' Katerina Lvovna said to Aksinya the cook, as she sat down to drink her tea on a carpet spread beneath a flowering apple tree. 'What do you think it all means, Aksinya?' she asked, wiping her saucer with the tea towel.

'What does what mean, ma'am?'

'I wasn't asleep, I'm sure I was wide awake, and a cat got in and started rubbing itself against me.'

'What are you talking about?'

'It's true. A cat got in.'

And Katerina Lvovna told Aksinya all about this cat that had somehow got into the bedroom.

'And why were you stroking it?'

'What do you mean – *why were you stroking it?* How would I know?'

'Well, it's all a riddle to me,' said the cook.

'And to me too.'

'It must mean that someone's heart has grown warm towards you, or something like that.'

'But what exactly?'

'No one, my friend, can tell you that – only that there's sure to be something.'

'I was dreaming about the moon – and then there was this cat,' Katerina Lvovna went on.

'The moon means a little one.'

Katerina Lvovna blushed.

'Wouldn't you like me to send for Sergei?' asked Aksinya, who was evidently hoping to be taken into Katerina Lvovna's confidence.

'All right then,' said Katerina Lvovna. 'Go and fetch him. He can have tea here with me.'

'All right, ma'am. I'll send him out to you,' said Aksinya, and waddled off towards the garden gate.

Katerina Lvovna told Sergei about the cat.

'But it's only a dream,' said Sergei.

'But why, Seryozha, have I never had a dream like that before?'

'There's many a thing that's never happened before. There was a time when I could do nothing but gaze after you and pine – but now I'm master of the whole of your white body!'

Sergei took Katerina Lvovna in his arms, whirled her round in the air and playfully threw her down on the soft carpet.

'Oh, you make my head spin,' said Katerina Lvovna. 'Sergei, come and sit with me for a moment,' she added, stretching herself out voluptuously.

Her young man bent down, came in under the low apple tree, which was awash with white blossom, and sat on the carpet at Katerina Lvovna's feet.

'So you were pining for me, were you, Seryozha?'

'How could I help pining?'

'How did you pine for me? Tell me what it was like.'

'How can I? How can I say what it is to pine? I longed for you.'

'But why didn't I sense you were longing for me? They say women sense things like that.'

Sergei said nothing.

'And why were you always singing,' Katerina went on, still

caressing him, 'if you were so unhappy without me? Well? It was you I used to hear singing outside the barn, wasn't it?'

'So what if I was singing? A mosquito sings all through its life, but that doesn't mean it's happy,' Sergei replied drily.

There was a pause. These confessions of Sergei's were music to Katerina Lvovna's ears.

She wanted to keep on talking, but Sergei frowned and said nothing.

'Look, Sergei – isn't this paradise? Simply paradise!' Katerina Lvovna exclaimed, looking up through branches thick with apple blossom at a clear pale-blue sky and a lovely full moon.

The light of the moon, filtering through the leaves and flowers of the apple tree, was playing over Katerina Lvovna's supine form, casting the most fantastical bright spots over her face and the whole of her body; the air was still; only the lightest of warm breezes ruffled the sleepy leaves, diffusing a delicate scent of flowering grasses and trees, instilling languor and indolence and conjuring up dark desires.

Getting no answer, Katerina Lvovna fell silent again and went on looking up at the sky through the pale pink apple blossom. Sergei was silent too; the sky, however, was of no interest to him. With both his arms flung round his knees, he was staring down at his boots.

The night was golden. Silence; light; delicate perfumes; and a benign, enlivening warmth. Beyond the ravine at the end of the orchard, someone began singing in a resonant voice; in the dense bird-cherry thicket by the fence, a nightingale trilled and burst into loud song; in a cage on a tall pole, a quail gave voice to its drowsy delirium; a sleek horse let out a lazy sigh from the other side of the stable wall; and a boisterous pack of dogs tore soundlessly across the pastureland beyond the fence, vanishing into the shapeless black shadow of the derelict salt warehouses.

Katerina Lvovna raised herself up on one elbow and looked at the tall orchard grass; the grass seemed to be playing with the light of the moon as it was filtered through the leaves and flowers of the apple trees. Capricious spots of light were turning the grass to gold, quivering and flickering over it like living butterflies of fire; or perhaps the grass under the trees had been caught in a net dropped by the moon and was being tossed from side to side.

'Oh, Seryozha my darling, how lovely it all is!' said Katerina Lvovna as she gazed around her.

Sergei looked around with indifference.

'What's the matter, Sergei? Why so gloomy? Are you tired of my love already?'

'Don't be silly,' said Sergei. Bending over her, he gave Katerina Lvovna a casual kiss.

'You're a deceiver, Seryozha,' said Katerina Lvovna. 'You're not to be trusted.'

'You must be talking about some other man,' Sergei replied calmly.

'Then why did you kiss me like that?'

Sergei said nothing.

'It's husbands and wives who kiss like that,' Katerina Lvovna went on, playing with his curls, 'and they do it to brush the dust off one another's lips. When you kiss me, I want you to kiss me so it makes the new blossom fall to the ground from this tree. Yes, like this,' she whispered, twining herself round her lover and kissing him passionately.

'Listen, Seryozha, there's something I want to ask you,' Katerina Lvovna began again a little later. 'Why does everyone say the same thing? Why do they all say you're a deceiver?'

'Who's been telling lies about me?'

'It's what people say.'

'Maybe the women I deceived were of no worth.'

'What were you doing with them then? Why were you loving worthless women?'

'What do you know about it? You think we decide these things in advance? It's temptation that does the work. You don't mean anything serious but you break the Lord's Commandment and then there's no getting away from a woman. There's love for you!'

'Listen to me, Seryozha! I know nothing about these other women, and I don't want to know anything about them. But you know very well how you turned my head and how you enticed me into this love of ours, and you know it was through your cunning as much as through my desire, and so if you ever deceive me, Seryozha, if you ever leave me for anyone else, then forgive me, my dear sweetheart, but I shan't be parted from you alive.'

Sergei gave a start.

'Katerina Lvovna! Light of my eyes!' he began. 'Can't you see how things are between you and me? You say I seem gloomy, but don't you ask yourself what it is that makes me so gloomy? What if my blood's all curdled with grief and it's drowning my heart?'

'Tell me, Sergei, tell me what grieves you!'

'What's there to tell? Any day now, God willing, your husband will be back home, and then – no more Sergei. He'll be out in the back yard again, sleeping beside the singers. He'll be looking up from the barn at a candle burning in Katerina Lvovna's bedroom as she plumps up the feather bed and lies down to rest with her lawful husband Zinovy Borisovich.'

'I don't think there'll be a lot of that,' said Katerina Lvovna, with a careless wave of the hand.

'Oh won't there? The way I see it myself, there most certainly will be. And I have a heart too, Katerina Lvovna. Yes, I can see the suffering that's in store for me.'

'Come on now. That's enough.'

Katerina Lvovna was pleased by this manifestation of Sergei's jealousy; she laughed, then went back to kissing him.

'But let me say once more,' Sergei began again, gently freeing his head from Katerina Lvovna's arms, which were bare to the shoulders, 'let me say once more that this lowly station of mine causes me to think many thoughts, and I think these thoughts not just once, and not just a dozen times. Yes, let me say, Katerina Lvovna, that were I your equal, were I some merchant or landowner, then I would never, no, never in my life, be parted from you. But you know very well, you know what my standing is compared to your own. Soon I shall see a man take you by your white hands and lead you into your bedroom and my poor heart will have to endure this and perhaps it will make me despise myself for the rest of my days. Katerina Lvovna! I'm not like those other fellows who don't care about anything if only they can have their way with a woman. I know what love is, and I can feel it sucking away at my heart like a black snake.'

'Why are you saying all this to me?' said Katerina Lvovna, now feeling sorry for Sergei.

'Katerina Lvovna! How can I not say it to you? How can I not? When your husband may already know everything, when he may already have heard the wildest of stories, when maybe as soon as tomorrow – not just some far-distant day – there'll be neither sight nor sound of Sergei in these parts, neither hide nor hair of Sergei?'

'No, no, don't even say such things, Seryozha! It won't be like that! It's not possible for me to be without you,' said Katerina Lvovna, trying to soothe him with her caresses. 'If there's going to be trouble, then either he dies or I die, but I'll never leave you.'

'No, Katerina Lvovna, that's not the way it'll be,' said Sergei, sadly shaking his head. 'The joy's gone out of my life because of this love of ours. If I loved a woman who didn't stand high above me, I'd be a happy man. How can your love for me ever remain constant? Does it bring you honour to be my mistress? I'd like to be your husband in the eyes of the holy and everlasting Church. I'd always understand that my place is beneath you, but at least I'd be able to make it plain and public how I have been rewarded for the deep respect I bear towards the woman I love.'

Katerina Lvovna was stupefied by these words of Sergei, by this jealousy of his and his desire to marry her – a desire that always pleases a woman, however intimate her relations with a man have already been. Katerina Lvovna was now ready to follow Sergei through hell and high water, to prison or cross. He had so enthralled her that her devotion to him was absolute. She was mad with happiness; her blood was on fire and she could no longer go on listening. She quickly pressed the palm of one hand against his lips, held his head to her breast and said, 'I know very well how to make a merchant of you and live with you as is right and proper. Only please don't upset me for nothing – there are bridges to cross, but they're still a long way ahead.'

And it was back to kisses and caresses.

In the silence of night, through his heavy slumber, the old steward in the nearby barn heard whispers and quiet giggles, as if naughty children were plotting how best to make fun of frail, decrepit old age; then came gay, ringing laughter, as if someone were being tickled by water nymphs from the lake. Splashing in and out of the moonlight, rolling about on the soft carpet, Katerina Lvovna was frolicking with her husband's young steward. Fresh white blossom from the curly-headed apple tree rained down on them, but in the end this rain ceased. The short summer night was passing; the moon had hidden behind the steep roofs of the high granaries and, turning ever dimmer, it was now looking askance at the earth; then there was a piercing duet from above the kitchen, followed by spitting, hissing and a great racket as two, or perhaps three, cats rolled off the roof and onto the pile of timber stacked against the wall.

'Let's go and sleep now,' Katerina Lvovna said slowly, as if worn out and battered. She got herself up off the carpet and, just as she was, in her shift and white petticoat, walked through the deathly silence of the yard. Walking behind her, Sergei was carrying the carpet and the blouse she had playfully thrown off.

7

Wearing only her shift, Katerina Lvovna had no sooner blown out the candle and lain down on the soft feather bed than she was fast asleep. After so much pleasure and love she was dead to the world; her arms slept, her legs slept, and yet, through this deep sleep, she once again heard the bedroom door open. With a soft thud like that of an old bast shoe,[1] the same huge tomcat landed beside her on the bed.

'What a confounded terror this cat is!' Katerina Lvovna thought wearily. 'I locked the door myself, I turned the key with my own hands, I shut the window – and here he is again. I must throw him out straight away.' Katerina Lvovna tried to get up, but her sleeping arms and legs refused to obey her; meanwhile the cat walked all over her, purring so strangely it was almost like human speech. This gave Katerina Lvovna goose pimples.

'Heavens!' she said. 'There's nothing for it – I must sprinkle the bed with holy water tomorrow. This cat that's taken to visiting me is a very queer cat indeed.'

But the cat went on purring and whirring, pushing his face against her and saying, 'Cat? Most certainly not! What makes you think I'm a cat? You know very well, Katerina Lvovna, that I'm not a tomcat but the honourable merchant Boris Timofeyevich. I'm just in a bad way at the moment because my guts inside me have been torn apart by a dish I was served by my daughter-in-law. That's what's made me shrink in size,' he purred on, 'and seem like a cat to anyone who doesn't understand who I really am. So, Katerina Lvovna, how are you getting along these days? Observing your vows faithfully, are you? I thought I'd come along from my grave to see how well you and Sergei Filipovich are keeping your husband's bed warm for him. Purr-purr, but I really can't see a thing. There's no need to be afraid of me: you see, those mushrooms made my eyes fall out. Look me in the eyes, my dear, don't be afraid!'

Katerina Lvovna looked – and screamed to high heaven. Once again the cat was lying between her and Sergei, but the head of this cat was the head of Boris Timofeyevich, every bit as big as the head of the late lamented; only instead of eyes there were two fiery circles spinning in opposite directions, spinning and spinning!

Sergei woke up, calmed Katerina Lvovna and went back to

sleep again, but she was now wide awake – which was just as well.

As she lay there with her eyes wide open, she heard what sounded like someone climbing over the gate. The dogs rushed to the gate but then they went quiet, as if it were someone they knew. A minute passed, there was a click from the iron lock and the front door opened. 'Either I'm dreaming or else my Zinovy Borisovich has come back. He's opened the door with his spare key,' thought Katerina Lvovna. She gave Sergei a quick shove.

'Listen, Seryozha,' she said. She was now leaning on one elbow, listening intently.

Someone was quietly climbing the stairs, moving cautiously, step by step, towards the locked door of the bedroom.

Katerina Lvovna leapt out of bed and opened the window. Sergei at once jumped out onto the gallery and put his legs round the post he had already slid down many a time.

'No, don't, don't! Lie down where you are. Don't go away,' Katerina Lvovna whispered. She threw Sergei's boots and clothes out of the window, then slipped back under the bedclothes and began to wait.

Sergei did as she said. Instead of sliding down the post, he lay down on the gallery, under the bast awning.

Meanwhile Katerina Lvovna could hear her husband; he had come up to the door and was listening outside, holding his breath. She could even hear the rapid beating of his jealous heart; what almost got the better of her, however, was not pity but malicious laughter.

'You're wasting your time!' she said to herself with a smile, her breathing as innocent as a baby's.

This went on for about ten minutes; in the end Zinovy Borisovich got bored with standing by the door and listening to his wife sleeping. He knocked.

Katerina Lvovna waited a moment and then called out sleepily, 'Who is it?'

'Your nearest and dearest,' replied Zinovy Borisovich.

'Is it you, Zinovy Borisovich?'

'Of course! Can't you tell?'

Katerina Lvovna jumped up again, let her husband into the bedroom and dived back into the warm bed.

'It turns a bit chilly just before dawn,' she said, pulling the blanket up over her.

Zinovy Borisovich looked round the room as he came in, said a prayer, lit a candle and looked round again.

'How have you been keeping?' he asked his wife.

'I've been all right,' said Katerina Lvovna. She sat up and pulled on a loose calico blouse. 'Shall I heat up the samovar?' she asked.

'Why bother? Just call Aksinya.'

Katerina Lvovna put on some slippers and ran out of the room. She was gone for half an hour. She lit the fire under the samovar and went quietly out onto the gallery for a word with Sergei.

'Here. Sit here!' she whispered.

'How long for?' answered Sergei, also in a whisper.

'Oh, how stupid you are! Sit here till I call you.'

And Katerina Lvovna sat him down in the same place as before.

From where he was, Sergei could hear everything that went on in the bedroom. Once again the door banged as Katerina Lvovna went in to her husband. Sergei could hear every word they said.

'Why have you been so long?' Zinovy Borisovich asked his wife.

'I was doing the samovar,' she replied calmly.

Then came a pause. Sergei could hear Zinovy Borisovich hanging up his frock coat on the rack. He washed, snorted, and splashed water in every direction. He asked for a towel. Then they started talking again.

'So how come you had to bury father?' asked Zinovy Borisovich.

'He died. He died, and we buried him.'

'How very strange!'

'Who's to say?' said Katerina Lvovna, clattering the cups about.

Zinovy Borisovich paced sadly up and down the room.

'And what have you been doing to pass the time?' he asked.

'Our joys are no secret. We don't go out of an evening – neither to balls nor theatres.'

'Nor, it seems, are you overjoyed to have your husband back home,' said Zinovy Borisovich, looking at her out of the corner of one eye.

'We're not young marrieds any more, to be dancing on air whenever we meet. What do you want from me? Here I am at your beck and call, running about the house at your pleasure.'

Katerina Lvovna ran off to fetch the samovar, slipped outside again, nudged Sergei and said, 'Mind you don't doze off, Seryozha!'

Sergei had no idea where all this was leading, but from then on he stayed alert and ready.

When Katerina Lvovna came back, she found Zinovy Borisovich kneeling on top of the coverlet; he was hanging his silver watch with its bead chain above the head of the bed.

'Why, Katerina Lvovna, do you make the bed up for two when you're all on your own?' he asked.

'I've been waiting for you,' she answered, looking at him calmly.

'For which we humbly thank you. And what's this doing on the bed?'

Sergei's thin woollen belt was lying on the sheet. Zinovy Borisovich picked it up and dangled it in front of his wife's eyes.

Katerina Lvovna didn't hesitate. 'I found it in the garden,' she said, 'and I used it to tie my skirt.'

'Yes!' said Zinovy Borisovich with peculiar emphasis. 'I've been hearing a few things about you and your skirts.'

'What is it you've heard?'

'About what you've been up to while I've been away.'

'I haven't been up to anything.'

'Well, we'll find out. We'll soon find out everything,' said Zinovy Borisovich, pushing his empty teacup towards his wife.

Katerina Lvovna said nothing.

'Yes, Katerina Lvovna. Whatever's been going on here, we'll soon get to the bottom of it,' said Zinovy Borisovich after another long pause, raising his eyebrows expressively.

'Your Katerina Lvovna's not so easily frightened. No, she's not easily frightened at all,' she replied.

'What! What!' shouted Zinovy Borisovich.

'Never mind,' said his wife. 'Forget it.'

'You watch your tongue! You've got an awful lot to say for yourself all of a sudden.'

'And why shouldn't I have a lot to say for myself?'

'You'd do better to look to how you behave.'

'And what's wrong with how I behave? Gossips gossip behind my back – and now I have to put up with insults from you! I like that!'

'It's not gossip, it's the truth – about you and your amours.'

'What amours?' yelled Katerina Lvovna, now flaring up in earnest.

'I know very well.'

'All right then, out with it.'

Zinovy Borisovich said nothing. Once again he pushed his empty cup towards his wife.

'Seems there's not a lot to say,' Katerina Lvovna said with contempt, tossing a teaspoon onto her husband's saucer. 'Go on then, tell me what people are saying. Who is this new lover of mine?'

'There's no hurry. You'll find out soon enough.'

'They've been making up stories about Sergei, haven't they?'

'We shall see, Katerina Lvovna, we shall see. No one has taken away my authority over you, and no one is going to take it away. You're going to tell me everything.'

'Oh, how I hate all this!' cried Katerina Lvovna. White as a sheet, she slipped out of the room.

'Here he is then,' she said a few moments later, leading Sergei into the room by his sleeve. 'Go on then. Ask what you like. But you may end up learning more than you bargained for.'

Zinovy Borisovich was by now quite bewildered. He looked at Sergei, who was leaning against the lintel, and he looked at his wife, who was sitting calmly on the edge of the bed with her arms crossed – and he couldn't for the life of him work out what was going to happen next.

'What the hell… You snake!' he finally managed to say, still in his armchair.

'You know everything anyway, so ask all you like,' said Katerina Lvovna insolently. 'You thought you could threaten

30

me with a beating,' she went on, with a sideways glance at Sergei, 'but you'll never ever lay a finger on me again. Yes, I decided what I was going to do with you long ago, before your threats – and I'm not about to change my mind now.'

'What's going on?' Zinovy Borisovich shouted at Sergei. 'Get out of here!'

'Well I never!' said Katerina Lvovna mockingly.

She quickly locked the door and dropped the key into her pocket. Then she went over to the bed and lolled there in her open blouse.

'Come on, dear Seryozha! Come here, my darling! Come to me!' she called out to the steward.

Sergei tossed back his curls and boldly sat down beside the mistress of the house.

'Good God! What – what are you doing, you savages?' shouted Zinovy Borisovich, his face going a dark red as he got up from the chair.

'What's the matter? Yes – look at him, feast your eyes on my bright-eyed falcon! Isn't he handsome?'

Katerina Lvovna burst out laughing and gave Sergei a passionate kiss.

Then she felt a stinging blow on one cheek, and Zinovy Borisovich was rushing towards the open window.

8

'Like that, is it? I'm well and truly grateful. I was waiting for something like that,' Katerina Lvovna cried out. 'Only now, my dear friend, I'm the one who's in charge here.'

In a single movement she pushed Sergei out of the way, jumped at Zinovy Borisovich from behind, and, before he could reach the window, grabbed him by the throat with her slender fingers and threw him to the ground like a sheaf of newly cut hemp.

Crashing down and smashing the back of his head against the floor, Zinovy Borisovich panicked. He had not expected a denouement as swift as this. Never before had his wife raised her hand against him; it was clear now that she would go to any lengths to be rid of him and that he was in terrible danger. Zinovy Borisovich understood all this in the instant of his fall and he did not cry out, knowing that his cries would go unheard and might only hasten his end. He looked round in silence, then let his eyes rest on his wife with an expression of rage, reproach and suffering; her fingers were still tightly gripping his throat.

Zinovy Borisovich made no attempt to defend himself. His fists were clenched and his arms lay stretched out on the floor, jerking spasmodically. One arm was free, the other pinned by Katerina Lvovna's knee.

'Hold him,' she whispered coolly to Sergei. Then she turned back to her husband.

Sergei sat on top of his master and pinned down his arms with his knees. But, just as he was about to slip his hands round his master's throat, beneath the hands of Katerina Lvovna, he let out a frenzied yell. Zinovy Borisovich had made a desperate effort; at the sight of his tormentor, his last strength galvanised by a wish for bloody revenge, he had freed his arms and seized hold of Sergei's black curls; like an animal, he sank his teeth into Sergei's throat. After a moment, however, Zinovy Borisovich let out a heavy groan and his head fell back.

Pale and scarcely breathing at all, Katerina Lvovna was standing over her husband and her lover. In her hand was a heavy cast-iron candlestick; she was holding it by the top end, the heavy base pointing downward. A thin stream of blood was flowing across Zinovy Borisovich's temple and cheek.

'A priest…' Zinovy Borisovich groaned dully. In horror he recoiled as far as he could from Sergei, who was still sitting on him. 'I want to confess,' he said still less clearly. He trembled as he looked out of the corner of one eye at the warm blood clotting under his hair.

'You'll do all right as you are,' whispered Katerina Lvovna. 'Get on with it,' she said to Sergei. 'Get a proper hold of his throat.'

Zinovy Borisovich began to wheeze.

Katerina Lvovna bent over her husband, pressed down with her hands on the hands clutching her husband's throat, and put her ear to his chest. After five silent minutes, she got up and said, 'All right, that'll do now.'

Sergei stood up too, puffing and panting. Zinovy Borisovich was dead; there was a gash in his temple and his throat had been crushed. Under his head, to the left, lay a small patch of blood. His wound, however, was now matted with hair, and the blood there had congealed.

Sergei carried Zinovy Borisovich to a cellar beneath the stone storeroom where he himself had so recently been confined by the late Boris Timofeyevich. Then he went back to the attic. Katerina Lvovna, her sleeves rolled up and the hem of her skirt tucked in, was scrubbing away with soap and bast at the bloody stain Zinovy Borisovich had left on the floor of his bedroom. The water had not yet gone cold in the samovar from which the master of the house had been warming his soul with poisoned tea, and she was able to wash away the blood completely.

Then she took a brass slop-basin and a well-soaped piece of bast.

'Go on, you hold the candle,' she said to Sergei as she walked over to the door. 'Lower down, closer to the floor,' she added, and she carefully examined each of the floorboards over which Zinovy Borisovich had been dragged on his journey down to the cellar.

Only in two places on the painted floor could she see spots of blood the size of cherries. Katerina Lvovna scrubbed them with the bast, and they disappeared. 'Creeping up on me like a thief, spying on your own wife – this'll teach you!' she said, standing up again and looking down towards the storeroom.

'That's it then,' said Sergei, trembling at the sound of his own voice.

When they got back to the bedroom, a first rosy streak of dawn had begun to show in the east, lightly gilding the blossoming apple trees and peeping through the green stakes of the orchard fence into Katerina Lvovna's room.

Crossing himself and yawning, a sheepskin jacket flung over his shoulders, the old steward was plodding across the yard from the barn to the kitchen.

Katerina Lvovna carefully pulled on the cord that opened the shutters and looked intently at Sergei, as if trying to see into his soul.

'Now you're a merchant,' she said, putting her white hands on Sergei's shoulders.

Sergei said nothing.

Sergei's lips were trembling, and he was shaking all over as if from fever. As for Katerina Lvovna, it was only her lips that were cold. Two days later, there were large calluses on Sergei's hands – from working with a heavy spade and a crowbar. Zinovy Borisovich, however, was by then so neatly buried away in his vault that, without the help of his widow or her lover, no one could have found him there until Judgement Day.

9

For some time Sergei wore a crimson kerchief round his neck, complaining that he had a swelling in his throat. But before the toothmarks on Sergei's neck had had time to heal, people began to wonder what had happened to Zinovy Borisovich. It was Sergei himself who brought up the subject most often. In the evening he would sit on the bench by the gate and say to the other young men, 'I can't help wondering, lads, why there's still no sign of our master.'

And the young lads all duly expressed their own wonderment.

Then came news from the mill: the master had hired some horses and set off back home long ago. The driver said that Zinovy Borisovich had seemed upset and had dismissed him in a rather strange fashion; about two miles from the town, near the monastery, he had got down from the cart, taken his bag and continued on foot. This strange story puzzled everyone still more.

Zinovy Borisovich had disappeared; that was all they knew.

Searches were carried out, but nothing was found; the merchant seemed to have vanished into thin air. The driver, who had by then been arrested, simply repeated his story: the merchant had got down from the cart near the river, just by the monastery, and had walked away. The mystery remained unsolved; in the meantime Katerina Lvovna took advantage of being a widow and began to live with Sergei more openly. People made up one story after another, saying that Zinovy Borisovich had been seen in such-and-such a place, then in some other place, but Zinovy Borisovich still didn't come back home and Katerina Lvovna knew better than anyone that he never would.

A month went by, a second month, then a third; Katerina Lvovna realised she was pregnant.

'The estate will be ours, Seryozha. There's going to be an heir,' she said. She went and spoke to the town council. She told them about her missing husband, said she was pregnant and complained that the business was getting into difficulties. She should be allowed to take over her husband's affairs.

A business couldn't just be left to go to rack and ruin, Katerina Lvovna was her husband's lawful wedded wife, there were no debts – so she must be allowed to take over. She took over.

Katerina Lvovna took charge of everything, and Sergei was no longer just plain Sergei but Sergei Filipovich. And then, like a bolt from the blue, came a new misfortune. The mayor received a letter from Lievin; the letter stated that Boris Timofeyevich had used not only his own capital to start up his business, but also that of his nephew Fyodor Zakharov Lyamin, a minor; matters, therefore, should be looked into and not left exclusively in the hands of Katerina Lvovna. The mayor passed this news on to Katerina Lvovna; and then, just a week later, an old woman arrived from Lievin together with a small boy.

'I am a first cousin of the late Boris Timofeyevich,' she announced, 'and this is my nephew Fyodor Lyamin.'

Katerina Lvovna invited them in.

Sergei, who had witnessed all this, turned white as a sheet.

'What's the matter?' asked Katerina Lvovna, noticing Sergei's deathly pallor as he followed the visitors into the house and stood in the vestibule, looking them up and down.

'Nothing,' said Sergei, turning back towards the entrance room. 'Only that men from Lievin can't keep from thievin'!' He sighed, went out and closed the door behind him.

'What are we going to do now?' Sergei Filipovich asked that evening, as he sat by the samovar with Katerina Lvovna. 'All our plans, Katerina Lvovna, have turned to ashes.'

'Why do you say that, Sergei?'

'Because everything's going to be divided up. We'll end up with such a paltry little business it won't be worth bothering with.'

'Won't our share be enough for you, Sergei?'

'That's not what upsets me. What upsets me is that I don't think we'll get much joy from this new state of affairs.'

'Why, Seryozha? Why won't there be any joy for us?'

'Because my love for you, Katerina Lvovna, makes me want to see you live like a real lady, not the way you've lived until now,' said Sergei Filipovich. 'But it's turning out the other way round: with the decrease in capital, we'll be worse off than ever.'

'But what does it matter, Sergei?'

'It may well be, Katerina Lvovna, that it doesn't matter to you, but to me, since I hold you in such esteem, and because of the way it will look to other people, who are always mean and envious, it will be terribly painful. You, of course, can think what you like, but it's only too clear to my judgement that, under these circumstances, I shall never be happy.'

And Sergei harped on about how, because of Fedya Lyamin, he himself was now the unhappiest of men, deprived as he was of the opportunity to elevate and exalt Katerina Lvovna in the eyes of all his fellow merchants. And he always ended by pointing out that, but for this Fedya, Katerina Lvovna would be giving birth to an heir, less than nine months since her husband had gone missing, that the entire estate would have been hers, and there would be no end to their happiness.

10

All of a sudden Sergei stopped talking about Fedya. And no
sooner had the name of Fedya Lyamin ceased to fall from
Sergei's lips than it lodged itself firmly in the mind and heart
of Katerina Lvovna. She grew so preoccupied that she even
turned cold towards Sergei. No matter whether she was asleep
in bed, out on business, or praying to God, one and the same
thought was always on her mind: 'It just isn't right! Why
should I lose my inheritance because of this boy? When I
think of all I've suffered, of the burden of sin I've taken upon
my soul – and then along he comes and takes everything from
me, just like that! And he isn't even a man – just a child, a mere
boy!'

The first frosts were setting in. There was, of course,
no news from anywhere about Zinovy Borisovich. Katerina
Lvovna continued to look preoccupied and grew bigger and
bigger; and much amazement was expressed in the town as to
how young Izmailova, who had always been barren and who
had been growing so thin she might have been wasting away,
could suddenly have begun to swell out in front. Meanwhile,
the young Fedya Lyamin, wearing only a light squirrel-fur
jacket, played about in the yard, smashing the cat-ice that
had formed in the ruts.

'What's got into you, Fyodor Zakharov?' Aksinya the cook
would call out as he ran across the yard. 'Poking about in
puddles – is that any way for a merchant's son to behave?'

But the young heir, whose presence so troubled Katerina
Lvovna and the object of her affections, played about as
serenely as a kid goat and slept still more serenely in the room
of the elderly aunt who was bringing him up; not for even a
moment did he suspect that he might be standing in anyone's

way or diminishing their happiness.

Then Fedya came down with the chickenpox, as well as catching a cold in the chest, and he was put to bed. At first he was treated with herbs; later they sent for a doctor.

The doctor paid frequent visits and prescribed medicines, to be given to the boy at regular intervals. Usually his aunt gave them to him herself; sometimes she would ask Katerina Lvovna.

'Dearest Katerina,' she would say, 'you're heavy with child, you're waiting for the will of God yourself. Do me a little kindness.'

Katerina Lvovna never refused. When the old woman went to the vigil to pray for 'young Fyodor, lying on his sickbed' or when she went to early mass so she could bring him back a particle of offering bread, Katerina Lvovna would sit beside him, giving him water to drink and making sure he took his medicine at the right time. And then one November evening, the eve of the Presentation of the Blessed Virgin, the old woman went out, meaning to attend both vespers and the vigil. She begged her dear Katerinushka to look after her dearest Fedyushka. By then the boy was on the mend.

When Katerina Lvovna went into his room, she found Fedya sitting up in bed in his squirrel-fur jacket, reading the *Lives of the Holy Fathers*.

'What are you reading, Fedya?' she asked, as she sat down in the armchair.

'I'm reading the *Lives*, Auntie.'

'Are they interesting?'

'Yes, Auntie, they're very interesting indeed.'

Katerina Lvovna leant her head on one hand and began to watch Fedya's gently moving lips. Suddenly it was as if demons had slipped their chains, and she was gripped once again by thoughts about how much evil this boy was doing her and how much better it would be if he were gone.

'Yes,' she said to herself. 'He's ill. He has to take medicine. And when you're ill… Yes, anything can happen. I can simply say the doctor gave him the wrong medicine.'

'I think it's time for your medicine, Fedya.'

'Thank you, Auntie.' He swallowed his spoonful of medicine. 'This book's very interesting, Auntie. It tells you all about the Saints.'

'Very good,' she said. She glanced coldly round the room; her eyes came to rest on the frost-patterned windows. 'It's time to close the shutters,' she said, and went out into the front room. From there she went to the dining hall, and then up to her attic, where she sat down.

Five minutes later, Sergei joined her there; he was wearing a fine sheepskin jacket trimmed with downy sealskin.

'Have the shutters been closed?' asked Katerina Lvovna.

'Yes,' said Sergei curtly, trimming the candle with a pair of scissors and then standing beside the stove.

They were silent.

'The vigil will go on a long time tonight, won't it?' asked Katerina Lvovna.

'Tomorrow's one of the great feast-days. The service will go on for ages,' Sergei replied.

There was another pause.

'I'd better go and look in on Fedya. He's alone,' said Katerina Lvovna, getting to her feet.

'Alone?' asked Sergei, looking at her intently.

'Yes,' she whispered. 'What of it?'

And something like lightning seemed to flash between their eyes, though neither of them said another word.

Katerina Lvovna went downstairs and walked through the

empty rooms. It was quiet everywhere; the icon lamps were shining peacefully; her own shadow slid about the walls; the shuttered windows were thawing out now and beginning to weep. Fedya was sitting and reading. Seeing Katerina Lvovna, he said, 'Auntie, please can you put this book away for me and give me the one from the icon case?'

Katerina Lvovna did as her nephew asked and gave him the book.

'Don't you want to go to sleep now, Fedya?'

'No, I'm going to wait for Babushka to come back.'

'Why?'

'She promised to bring me a piece of bread that's been blessed.'

Katerina Lvovna went pale; her own child had stirred inside her for the first time, beneath her heart, and a chill passed through her. She stood in the middle of the room and then went out, rubbing her cold hands together.

'Now,' she whispered, as she went quietly into her bedroom and found Sergei still standing beside the stove.

'What?' he asked, almost inaudibly. He cleared his throat.

'He's alone.'

Sergei raised his eyebrows and began to breathe heavily.

'Come on,' said Katerina Lvovna, turning abruptly towards the door.

Sergei quickly took off his boots and asked, 'Do we need anything?'

'No,' said Katerina Lvovna under her breath. And, taking Sergei by the hand, she led him quietly out of the room.

11

When Katerina Lvovna entered his room for a third time, the sick boy shuddered and dropped his book on his knees.

'What's the matter, Fedya?'

'Oh Auntie, something frightened me,' he answered, giving her a troubled smile and curling himself up in a corner of the bed.

'What was it?'

'Who was with you just now, Auntie?'

'What do you mean, darling? There wasn't anyone with me.'

'Are you sure?'

The boy stretched out towards the foot of the bed. Screwing up his eyes, he stared at the doorway through which his auntie had just entered. He calmed down.

'I must have imagined it,' he said.

Katerina Lvovna stopped for a moment, leaning one elbow against the headboard of the boy's bed.

Fedya looked up at his auntie and said that she looked terribly pale.

By way of an answer, Katerina Lvovna just pretended to cough and looked expectantly towards the door into the front room. But there was no sound, just a creak from one of the floorboards.

'Auntie, I'm reading the life of my guardian angel, St Theodore Stratilates. How well he served God!'[2]

Katerina Lvovna stood there without a word.

'Do you want to sit down, Auntie, and I'll read to you?' Fedya asked affectionately.

'Yes, in a moment, but first let me trim the wick of the icon lamp in the hall,' said Katerina Lvovna. She hurried out.

There was the very faintest of whispering in the front room;

amid the general silence, however, this reached the boy's sharp ears.

'Auntie, what is it? Who are you whispering to?' the boy cried out, with tears in his voice. 'Come here, Auntie, I'm frightened!' he called a moment later, still more tearfully. Then, thinking she was speaking to him, he heard Katerina Lvovna say, 'Now!'

'What are you frightened of?' Katerina Lvovna asked a little hoarsely, striding into the room and standing beside the bed so as to block the boy's view of the doorway. 'Lie down now.'

'But I don't want to, Auntie.'

'No, Fedya, you must do as I say. It's time you lay down.'

'But why, Auntie? I really don't want to.'

'Lie down now, lie down,' Katerina Lvovna repeated, in a voice that had begun to tremble. Seizing him under the armpits, she laid him down with his head on the pillow.

Just then Fedya let out a terrible scream. He had glimpsed Sergei, pale and barefoot.

Katerina Lvovna put her hand over the boy's mouth, which had dropped open in horror, and shouted, 'Quick, hold him still, so he can't struggle!'

Sergei seized hold of Fedya's arms and legs while Katerina Lvovna, in one movement, covered the child's face with a large feather pillow and threw herself across it, her firm resilient bosom pressing down on the pillow.

For a while the room was quiet as the grave.

'He's dead,' whispered Katerina Lvovna. Hardly had she got to her feet to put everything in order when the walls of the silent house, that had witnessed so many crimes, were shaken by deafening blows; windows rattled, floors shook, and the chains of the hanging icon lamps sent fantastic shadows flitting across the walls.

Sergei shuddered and took to his heels; Katerina Lvovna rushed after him, pursued by a terrible uproar. It was as if this house of sin were being rocked to its foundations by unearthly powers.

Katerina Lvovna was concerned that Sergei, driven by terror, might run out into the yard and betray himself through his panic, but he rushed straight up towards the attic.

As he ran up the stairs in the dark, Sergei struck his forehead against a half-open door and fell back down again with a groan; he was out of his mind with superstitious terror. 'Zinovy Borisovich, Zinovy Borisovich!' he muttered – and flew head over heels down the staircase, knocking Katerina Lvovna off her feet and taking her with him.

'Where?' she asked.

'There, just above us, flying by with a sheet of iron! There he goes again! Oh! Oh!' cried Sergei. 'He's thundering, he's thundering!'

It was clear that many hands were knocking at each of the windows that looked onto the street, and that someone was trying to break down the door.

'You idiot! Get up, you idiot!' shouted Katerina Lvovna. With these words she darted back to Fedya, settled his dead head on the pillow in as natural a position as possible, and resolutely opened the door, through which a large crowd was trying to force its way in.

It was a terrible sight. People were laying siege to the porch; beyond them, armies of strangers were climbing over the high fence into the yard; the street was filled with the hubbub of voices.

Before Katerina Lvovna had time to think, she was forced back inside, crushed by the crowd that had gathered around the porch.

12

The alarm had been raised in the following manner. Though only the capital of a small district, the town where Katerina Lvovna lived was an important centre of industry, and on the eve of each of the twelve great feasts its churches were always packed with people; as for the churches named after the feast being celebrated, there was barely room for an apple to fall even in their churchyards. It was the custom on these days for there to be a choir made up of young men from the merchant classes, led by a precentor who was also a lover of the art of singing.

Our people are pious and enthusiastic churchgoers, and they are not without a sense of art. Ecclesiastical magnificence and harmonious 'organ-like' singing constitute one of their highest and purest pleasures. When a choir is singing, almost half the town will gather to listen; above all, you are sure to find young men of the merchant and artisan classes: stewards, shop assistants and errand-boys, workers from the mills and factories, even the merchants themselves and their better halves – all will crowd together into a single church, happy if they can just stand in the porch or listen outside a window, in blazing heat or biting frost, as the deep bass thunders away and a high tenor pours out the most capricious of grace notes.

The parish church nearest to the Izmailovs' house was dedicated to the Presentation in the Temple of the Blessed Virgin and so, on the eve of this feast, while the events we have just related were taking place, the young men of the entire town had assembled there. When the service came to an end, they left in a noisy crowd, discussing the merits of the well-known tenor and the unfortunate awkwardnesses of the no less well-known bass.

Not all of them, however, were discussing the subtleties of the art of singing; some had other things on their minds.

'Hey, I've heard some fine stories about that young Izmailova,' said a young machinist, recently arrived from St Petersburg to take care of a merchant's steam mill, as they approached her house. 'I've heard there's love going on all day long between her and her young steward!'

'There's none of us hasn't heard stories about Izmailova,' said a sheepskin coat covered in blue cloth. 'Seems she hasn't been to church even today.'

'Church? That bitch has been rolling in filth for so long she fears neither conscience nor God nor the eyes of others.'

'Look – a light,' said the machinist, pointing to a chink between the shutters.

'Let's have a peek! Let's see what they're up to!' people called out.

The machinist climbed up on the shoulders of two of his comrades and had barely put his eye to the chink when he yelled out, 'Help! Murder! Someone's being suffocated!'

And the machinist desperately began banging at the shutter. A dozen or so other men at once followed his example, leaping up and hammering with their fists on the other windows.

The crowd grew bigger every moment and, as we have seen, the Izmailovs' house was besieged.

'I saw it myself, I saw it with my own eyes,' the machinist was to testify later, standing over Fedya's corpse. 'They'd forced the boy down on the bed and the two of them were suffocating him.'

Sergei was taken to the police station that evening; Katerina Lvovna was led upstairs to her attic and two policemen were stationed outside the door.

The cold in the Izmailovs' house was unbearable; the stoves

46

were not lit and, what with the crowds of inquisitive townsfolk who kept thronging in, the front door never stayed closed for even a minute. Everyone wanted to look not only at Fedya lying in his coffin but also at another large coffin, its tightly closed lid covered by a broad pall... Across Fedya's forehead lay a white satin band, concealing the red scar left by a post-mortem examination carried out on his skull. This had confirmed that Fedya had indeed been suffocated and, when Sergei was led before the corpse, the priest's very first words about the Last Judgement and the punishment of the unrepentant had reduced him to tears; not only did he at once confess to the murder of Fedya but he also begged them to dig up the body of Zinovy Borisovich, who had had no proper funeral. The corpse of Katerina Lvovna's husband had been lying in dry sand and had not entirely decomposed; it was disinterred and laid in a large coffin. To universal horror, Sergei named the young mistress of the house as his accomplice in both crimes. Katerina Lvovna herself had refused to answer any questions, saying only, 'I know nothing, I know absolutely nothing.' Sergei was asked to repeat his statement in her presence. After hearing his confession, she looked at him in mute amazement but without anger and said coolly, 'If that's what he's taken it into his head to tell you, then why should I deny it? I killed them.'

'Why?' they asked.

'For him,' she said, pointing to Sergei, who was looking down at the floor.

The two accused were taken to prison, and this terrible case, which had provoked such universal outrage, was soon settled in the criminal court. At the end of February, Sergei and Katerina Lvovna, the widow of a merchant of the third guild,[3] both received the same sentence: a flogging in the market square, to be followed by penal servitude in Siberia. On a frosty morning at the beginning of March, the executioner counted off the appointed number of blue-and-crimson weals on Katerina Lvovna's bare white back, then gave Sergei's shoulders their fair share of the lash and stamped his handsome face with the three marks of a convict.

Throughout this scene, for some reason, Sergei evoked a great deal more sympathy than Katerina Lvovna. Dirty and bloodstained, he stumbled as he descended from the black scaffold; Katerina Lvovna, however, walked down quite steadily, concerned only to prevent her thick shirt and coarse prison coat from touching her lacerated back.

And even when, in the prison hospital, she was presented with her baby, she merely said, 'Oh, who cares!' and, without the least sound of complaint, collapsed face down on the hard prison bed.

13

The day that Sergei and Katerina Lvovna's detachment of convicts set off was a spring day only according to the calendar; the sun in the heavens was – as people say – shining brightly but warming little.

Katerina Lvovna's child had been handed over to the care of the old woman, Boris Timofeyevich's cousin, since, being considered the legitimate son of the felon's murdered husband, this infant was now sole heir of the Izmailov estate. Katerina Lvovna was satisfied with this and gave up her child with complete indifference. Her love for the father, like the love of many excessively passionate women, did not in any way carry over to the child.

But then nothing now existed for her at all, neither light nor dark, neither bad nor good, neither sorrow nor joys. She understood nothing and loved no one, not even herself. Hoping once again to see her dear Seryozha, she was living only for the moment of their departure for Siberia; as for the child, she never gave him a thought.

Katerina Lvovna's hopes were not disappointed; his face branded, his legs shackled with heavy chains, Sergei passed through the prison gates with the same group that she had been assigned to herself. Human beings accustom themselves as best they can to any situation, however awful, and they retain the power to pursue their meagre joys. Katerina Lvovna, however, did not need to accommodate herself to anything; she could see her Sergei, and with him beside her even the road to Siberia would flower with happiness.

There were only a few things of value in Katerina Lvovna's cloth bag, and still less ready money. What little she had, however, she soon gave away; long before they reached Nizhny Novgorod, she had given everything to the guards in exchange for permission to walk beside Sergei or to embrace him for an hour in the darkness of night, standing in some cold corner of a narrow transit-prison corridor.

Katerina Lvovna's now branded lover, however, had somehow become most unaffectionate. Whatever he said to her, he said curtly and crossly; and he set no great store on the secret trysts for the sake of which she herself went without food and drink and would part with twenty-five-kopek pieces from her slender purse. More than once he even said, 'What's the good of our meeting just to polish the corners of corridors with our backs? Why give money to the guard when you could be giving it to me?'

'But Seryozhenka, I didn't pay much – only twenty-five

kopeks!' she would reply.

'Only twenty-five kopeks! I suppose people give you any number of coins on the road. You're certainly free enough with them yourself!'

'But at least we get to see one another, Seryozha!'

'And what good does that do us? After the torment we've been through, I feel like cursing my whole life. As for lovers' trysts…'

'Nothing matters except you, Seryozha. All I want is to see you.'

'Oh, what nonsense you talk,' Sergei would reply.

Sometimes words like these made Katerina Lvovna bite her lips till they bled, and sometimes, in the darkness of these nocturnal meetings, tears of anger and resentment would well up in her usually dry eyes; yet she put up with everything, never answered back and went on trying to deceive herself.

And so, with their relations on this new footing, they reached Nizhny Novgorod. Here their group was joined by a detachment that had arrived by the Moscow road; it, too, was on its way to Siberia.

There were people of all kinds in this large detachment, but two of the women were especially striking: one was a soldier's wife from Yaroslavl by the name of Fiona[4], a tall magnificent woman with a thick plait of black hair and languorous brown eyes veiled by thick lashes; the other was a little seventeen-year-old blonde with sharply defined features, delicate rosy skin, a tiny little mouth, dimples on her fresh cheeks and golden curls that strayed capriciously onto her forehead from beneath her convict's headscarf. This girl was known as little Sonya, or Sonetka.[5]

The beautiful Fiona was easygoing and lazy. Everyone in the detachment knew her, and none of the men were especially gratified if they won her favours or upset if they witnessed her favours being granted to another.

'Our Fiona's a good girl, she never turns anyone down,' the convicts agreed jokingly.

Sonetka, however, was different.

'Slippery as an eel,' they said. 'Dances about beside you, but she's not easy to catch.'

Sonetka had taste and she liked to pick and choose; she was, in fact, very choosy indeed. She wanted passion to be served up to her not as some common or garden dish, but with a highly spiced, piquant sauce, with sufferings and sacrifice. Fiona, on the other hand, was the image of Russian simplicity – too lazy even to tell a man to get lost and knowing nothing except that she is a woman. Such women are highly prized by gangs of thieves, convict detachments and St Petersburg social-democratic communes.

The presence of these two women in the same detachment as Sergei and Katerina Lvovna was to spell tragedy for the latter.

14

The moment they set out from Nizhny Novgorod towards Kazan, Sergei quite openly began making a play for Fiona, the soldier's wife – and he met with success. The languid and beautiful Fiona did not make Sergei suffer any more than, with her goodness of heart, she had ever made any man suffer. At their third or fourth halting-place Katerina Lvovna had a word at twilight with one of the guards and bribed him into allowing her to see Sergei; she then lay there awake, waiting for the guard to come and give her a quiet nudge and whisper, 'Off with you now!' The door opened – and a woman darted out into the corridor; the door opened a second time – and another woman jumped down from her place on the bed-boards and followed the guard out; at last someone tugged at the coat lying on top of Katerina Lvovna. She quickly got up from the bed-boards, which had been worn smooth by the sides of countless convicts, threw the coat over her shoulders, and nudged the guard waiting in front of her.

As Katerina Lvovna walked down a corridor lit only by one dim oil lamp, she stumbled over two or three couples whom it was quite impossible to make out except from close to. As she approached the men's section, she heard muffled laughter coming through the spyhole cut in the door.

'A grand time those pigs are having!' muttered the guard. Taking Katerina Lvovna by the shoulders, he pushed her into a corner and made off.

Katerina Lvovna groped about her. One hand touched a coat and a beard; the other – the hot face of a woman.

'Who is it?' Sergei asked under his breath.

'What – who – who's *that*?'

In the dark Katerina Lvovna snatched the scarf from her rival's head. The latter slipped to one side, took to her heels, tripped over someone in the corridor and fell.

There was a burst of hearty laughter from the other men.

'Bastard!' whispered Katerina Lvovna, whipping Sergei on the face with the ends of the scarf she had pulled off his new girlfriend's head.

Sergei would have hit back, but Katerina Lvovna shot off down the corridor and returned to her section. The laughter following her from the men's section, however, was so loud that the guard in the corridor, who had been standing apathetically by the oil lamp and spitting onto the toecap of one boot, raised his head and bellowed, 'Quiet!'

Katerina Lvovna lay down without a word and hardly moved all night. Wanting to say to herself, 'I don't love him,' she felt she loved him more ardently than ever. And before her eyes she kept seeing the palm of his hand trembling beneath *that woman's* head, and his other arm embracing her hot shoulders.

Poor Katerina Lvovna burst into tears, involuntarily praying for that palm to be lying beneath her own head and that other arm to be embracing her own violently trembling shoulders.

'Come on now, give me back my headscarf,' said Fiona in the morning, waking Katerina Lvovna from her sleep.

'So it was you, was it?'

'Give it back, please!'

'Why are you trying to come between us?'

'I'm not coming between you – he means nothing to me. It's nothing to get worked up about.'

Katerina Lvovna thought for a moment, took from under her pillow the headscarf she had snatched during the night, threw it at Fiona and turned her face to the wall.

She felt calmer now.

'Pah!' she said to herself. 'Why should I feel jealous? To hell with the painted bitch. She's no equal of mine – it makes me sick even to think of her.'

'Listen, Katerina Lvovna,' said Sergei, after they had set off the following morning. 'I'd like you to get it into your head, first, that I'm no Zinovy Borisovich, and second, that you're no longer the wife of an important merchant. It's no use being pigheaded – beggars can't be choosers!'

Katerina Lvovna said nothing, and for an entire week she walked beside Sergei without the two of them exchanging so much as a word or a look. Being the injured party in this first quarrel she had ever had with Sergei, she stood on her dignity; she had no wish to make the first move herself.

In the meantime Sergei began courting little blonde Sonetka. He would bow to her with his 'most respectful greetings'; he would smile at her; if she passed by, he would try to put his arms round her and hug her. Katerina Lvovna saw all this, and it enraged her.

'Perhaps I really should try and make it up with Sergei?' she would wonder, staggering along, not seeing the ground beneath her feet.

But pride now made it harder than ever for her to make a move. And Sergei was chasing more and more determinedly after Sonetka, and everyone was beginning to see that the inaccessible blonde, whom no one could get their hands on even when she danced about beside them, had all of a sudden grown tamer.

'You were mad at me,' Fiona said to Katerina Lvovna one day, 'but what harm did I ever do you? I had my chance, and it's gone now. But if I were in your shoes, I'd keep an eye on that Sonetka.'

'To hell with my pride,' Katerina Lvovna admonished herself, 'I really must make it up with him.' All she could think of now was how best to achieve this.

It was Sergei himself who helped her out of her difficulty.

'Lvovna!' he called out to her during one of their halts. 'Come and see me for a moment tonight. I've got something to say to you.'

Katerina Lvovna said nothing.

'Not still cross with me, are you? Won't you come?'

Once again Katerina Lvovna made no answer.

But Sergei, like everyone else watching Katerina Lvovna, noticed that, as they approached the transit prison, she edged closer and closer to the senior guard in order to slip him the seventeen kopeks she had collected in alms on the way.

'I'll give you another ten as soon as I've got them,' she said pleadingly.

The guard tucked the money away in the cuff of his coat sleeve and said, 'All right then.'

When the negotiations were over, Sergei cleared his throat and winked at Sonetka.

'Oh, Katerina Lvovna!' he said, embracing Katerina on the steps of the transit prison. 'Yes, lads, this one's in a class of her own. There's not a woman in the world who can outshine her.'

Katerina Lvovna blushed, choking with happiness.

Hardly had night fallen when the door gently opened and she went rushing out; trembling all over, she groped her way down the dark corridor in search of Sergei.

'My Katya!' said Sergei, embracing her.

'Oh my wicked man!' Katerina Lvovna replied through her tears, putting her lips to his.

A sentry came down the corridor, stopped for a moment, spat on his boots, then walked on; from the other side of a door came the snores of weary convicts; a mouse gnawed at a feather; crickets beneath the stove tried their best to outchirp one another – and Katerina Lvovna was in seventh heaven.

But ecstasies tire, and prose always follows.

'I'm fair dying of pain,' Sergei lamented, sitting with Katerina Lvovna on the floor, in a corner of the corridor. 'Yes, my bones are aching from my ankles right the way up to my knees.'

'But what can we do about it, my darling?' she asked, trying to make herself comfortable under the skirts of his coat.

'Should I try and get myself into hospital in Kazan?'

'Seryozha – how can you say such a thing?'

'But this pain will be the death of me.'

'Staying behind while I go on – how could you?'

'But what can I do?' Sergei continued a moment later. 'The chains grind and grind. Soon they'll be eating right into the bone. Maybe if I had a pair of woollen stockings…'

'Stockings? But Seryozha, I've got a pair of new stockings myself!'

'Oh no, I couldn't…'

Without saying another word, Katerina Lvovna darted away, scattered everything from her bag onto the bed-boards and came rushing back to Sergei with a pair of thick blue Bolkhov woollen stockings with brightly coloured arrows on the sides.[6]

'Now I'll be fine,' said Sergei, as he said goodnight to Katerina Lvovna and took her last pair of stockings.

Happy now, Katerina Lvovna went back to her place on the bed-boards and fell fast asleep.

She did not hear Sonetka go out into the corridor, nor did she hear her return only shortly before dawn.

All this happened when they were just two days from Kazan.

15

As they left the stuffy transit prison, the convicts were greeted by a cold miserable day, with a gusty wind and rain that was turning to snow. Katerina Lvovna was in good spirits; the moment she took her place in the column, however, she went green and started to tremble all over. Her eyes saw only darkness; every joint in her body was weak and aching. In front of her stood Sonetka – wearing a familiar pair of blue woollen stockings with bright arrows.

As they set off, Katerina Lvovna seemed more dead than alive; her eyes, however, followed Sergei with a terrible and unblinking stare.

At the first halt, she walked calmly up to him, whispered 'You bastard!' and spat into his eyes. Sergei would have attacked her, but he was held back.

'Just you wait!' he said, as he wiped his face.

'Aha!' laughed the other convicts. 'That one's not frightened of you, is she?' Sonetka's laughter was especially merry; this kind of affair was right up her street.

'You'll pay for this!' Sergei warned Katerina Lvovna.

Lying in troubled sleep that night on the bed-boards of yet another transit prison, worn out and broken in spirit by the long distance and the bad weather, Katerina Lvovna did not hear two men slip into the women's section. As they came in, Sonetka sat up and silently pointed to Katerina Lvovna; then she lay down again and wrapped herself in her coat.

Katerina Lvovna's own coat suddenly went flying over her head; and her back, covered only by a coarse shirt, felt the lash of the thick end of a double-plaited rope being swung with all the might of a peasant's arm.

Katerina Lvovna shrieked, but her voice was stifled by the coat over her head. She struggled to break free, but to no avail: a burly convict was sitting on her shoulders and pinning down her arms.

'Fifty,' a voice said at last; it was easy enough to recognise this voice as Sergei's. The nocturnal visitors disappeared straight away.

Katerina Lvovna freed her head and jumped up. No one was there; all she could hear was a woman giggling beneath her coat. Katerina Lvovna recognised Sonetka's laugh.

The hurt she had suffered was beyond all measure; nor was there any measure to the fury now seething in her heart. She rushed blindly forward – and she collapsed blindly onto the breast of Fiona; Fiona supported her as she fell.

On this full bosom, which had so recently gratified her depraved and faithless lover, she now sobbed out her unbearable grief, pressing herself against her plump and stupid rival as a child presses itself against its mother. They were equal now: both valued at the same price, both discarded.

They were equal: Fiona, who accepted whatever Chance brought her; and Katerina Lvovna, acting her role in the drama of Love.

Nothing, however, could hurt Katerina Lvovna now. Having shed all her tears, she stood stock-still and waited for the roll call with wooden calm.

The drum was beating – tat-tararat-tat. Fettered and unfettered, the convicts poured out into the yard: Sergei, Fiona, Sonetka, Katerina Lvovna, an Old Believer shackled to a Jew, a Pole on the same chain as a Tartar.

They all crowded together, got themselves into some kind of order and set off.

A joyless picture: a handful of people, torn from the world and deprived of any last shadow of hope, sinking into the cold black mud of a dirt road. Everything round about is ugly and terrible: infinite mud, a grey sky, wet leafless willows with sullen crows perched on their spreading branches. The wind howls and gusts, moans and rages.

These hellish, heart-rending sounds complete the horror of the scene; in them echoes the advice given to Job by his wife: 'Curse the day that thou wast born, and die.'[7]

Those who do not wish to hear the meaning of these words, those who, even amid such sorrow, are frightened rather than charmed by the thought of death, must do what they can to drown out these howling voices with something still more hideous. The simple man understands this only too well; giving free rein to all his brutish simplicity, he plays the fool; he jeers at himself, he jeers at others, he jeers at every emotion. Never noted for tenderness, at moments like this he becomes especially evil.

'Hello, madam merchant, is Your Honour in good health?' Sergei said mockingly to Katerina Lvovna. The village where they had spent the night had just disappeared behind a wet hillock.

With these words he turned to Sonetka, made room for her under his coat and began to sing in a high falsetto:

> *'In the dark inside the window I glimpse a fair head.*
> *My troublemaker's awake, my tormentor's not sleeping.*
> *Let me throw my coat over you so no one can see.'*

Sergei embraced Sonetka in front of everyone and gave her a smacking kiss.

Katerina Lvovna saw everything and saw nothing; she might have been no longer alive. People nudged her, remarking on the way Sergei was carrying on with Sonetka. Katerina Lvovna had become a laughing stock.

'Leave her alone,' Fiona kept saying, doing her best to defend the stumbling Katerina Lvovna whenever one of the convicts poked fun at her. 'The woman's ill. Can't you see, you devils?'

'Must have got her tootsies wet,' joked a young convict.

'She had a delicate upbringing,' said Sergei. 'She's from a merchant family. Now if only she had a pair of warm stockings,' he went on, 'she'd be all right.'

Katerina Lvovna appeared to wake up.

'Bastard!' she said, suddenly cracking. 'Go on, you bastard, jeer all you like!'

'Oh no, madam merchant, I'm not jeering. It's just that Sonetka here has some mighty fine stockings to sell and I thought they might be what a merchant's wife fancies.'

A number of people laughed. Katerina Lvovna marched on, like an automaton.

The weather got worse and worse. Wet flakes of snow fell from the grey clouds covering the sky; melting as they touched the ground, they made the mud still deeper and more impassable. At last a dark leaden band came into view; beyond it nothing could be made out at all. This was the Volga. A stiff wind was blowing across the river; dark gaping waves slowly rose and fell; the wind drove them this way and that way.

Soaked to the bone and shivering, the convicts went slowly up to the pier and stopped to wait for the ferry.

The ferry drew in, all dark and wet; the crew settled the convicts on board.

'I've heard there's vodka for sale here on this boat,' said one convict. Wet flakes of snow were still falling on the ferry, which had put off from the pier and was now tossing about on the river's ever-choppier waves.

'Yes, a drop or two wouldn't go down badly,' said Sergei. To amuse Sonetka, he went on tormenting Katerina Lvovna. 'I say, madam merchant, won't you treat us to a drop of vodka for old time's sake? Don't be mean! O my dear one, remember our former love! Remember, O my joy, what good times we had together! Remember how you and I delighted in the long autumn nights, how we dispatched your family to eternal rest without benefit of clergy.'

Katerina Lvovna was shivering with cold. As well as this cold, which had penetrated through her clothes and to the very marrow of her bones, other forces were at work within her. Her head was burning as if in fever; her pupils were dilated, animated by a sharp wandering brilliance yet fixed on the rolling waves.

'I could do with some vodka too – this cold's more than I can bear!' Sonetka chimed in.

'Please, madam merchant! Go on, stand us a drink!' teased Sergei.

'Have you no conscience?' said Fiona, shaking her head reproachfully.

'You should show some shame,' said Gordyushka, another of the convicts.

'At least in front of other people!' said Fiona.

'Shut up, you old slut!' Sergei shouted back. 'Shame? What have I got to be ashamed of? I don't believe I ever did love her… Her ugly old mug means less to me now than one of Sonetka's old shoes. And that's all there is to it. Filthy bitch! She can go love Gordyushka – mean-mouthed Gordyushka.' He looked round and happened to see a puny guard wearing a felt cloak and a military cap with a cockade. He went on, 'Or maybe she should try her charms on this here officer. At least she'll be out of the rain under his burka.'

'And then we could call her madam officer,' said Sonetka.

'Yes! And she wouldn't be short of money for stockings.'

Katerina Lvovna made no attempt to defend herself; she just kept moving her lips and staring more and more intently at the waves. In between Sergei's vile jokes she could hear some kind of groan or rumble coming from the heaving, crashing waves. Out of one breaking wave appeared the blue head of Boris Timofeyevich, and out of another – her husband,

61

swaying from side to side. In his arms he held Fedya, whose head was hanging down against his chest. Katerina Lvovna tried to remember a prayer; she moved her lips, but all they could whisper was 'What good times we had together, and how we delighted in the long autumn nights. And how, through terrible death, we robbed people of the light of day.'

Katerina Lvovna trembled. Now wilder than ever, her wandering eyes were focused on a single point. Once, twice, her arms stretched out towards somewhere in space, then dropped back again. Suddenly she began to rock and sway; without taking her eyes off the dark waves, she seized Sonetka by the legs and, in a single movement, leapt overboard, taking Sonetka with her.

Everyone froze in astonishment.

Katerina Lvovna appeared on the crest of a wave, then disappeared; another wave revealed Sonetka.

'A boat-hook! Throw them a boat-hook!' people shouted.

A heavy boat-hook flew out on a long rope and fell into the water. Sonetka had disappeared. A few seconds later, as the current swept her away from the ferry, she flung her arms up in the air again, but just then Katerina Lvovna appeared from another wave, rose almost waist-high above the water and flung herself at Sonetka like a powerful pike attacking a roach. Neither of them was seen again.

NOTES

1. Bast, the inner bark of birch and linden trees, was used to make footwear, matting and many other things.

2. St Theodore Stratilates was a powerful general under the Roman tetrarch Licinius (r. 308–25 AD). He was secretly a Christian, and, at a pageant held in his honour by Licinius, he destroyed a number of gold pagan idols. Theodore was brutally tortured and martyred for his faith, and was subsequently canonised and proclaimed the patron saint of soldiers.

3. The wealthiest merchants belonged to the first guild, the next most wealthy to the second guild, the least wealthy to the third guild. Members of the first and second guilds, unlike members of the third guild, were exempt from physical punishment.

4. A Russian dictionary gives this as a folk variant of Khiona, derived from the Greek word for snow: *chion*. It is possible that Leskov was familiar with the Scottish name. In either case, however, the significance of the name is unclear.

5. Sonya is a common diminutive of the name Sofya. Sonetka, however, is extremely uncommon. Leskov is playing on the word's other meaning: a small hand bell. Everything about her is bright and bell-like.

6. These stockings, despite the arrows, have nothing to do with prison uniform. Bolkhov is a small town, known for its handicrafts, not far from the town where Katerina Lvovna had lived as a married woman.

7. Job II.9. The words spoken by Job's wife were, in fact, 'Curse God, and die.'

Nikolai Leskov was born in the village of Gorokhovo, in Oryol province, western Russia, in 1831. His family was relatively poor, and his education was undertaken first at the home of his formidable uncle Strakhov and later at the Oryol Gymnasium. After abandoning his formal education at the age of fifteen, Leskov worked for eight years as a clerk in the Kiev army recruiting office, during which time he read widely, and developed a detailed knowledge of many subjects, most notably Russian Orthodoxy. Whilst in Kiev, Leskov met and married Olga Vasilevna Smirnova, the daughter of a local merchant. The marriage produced two children, but was ultimately unsuccessful, and Olga's erratic behaviour eventually led to her committal for insanity.

In 1857 Leskov and his family moved to north-eastern Russia, where he took employment in his British uncle's firm. Leskov was obliged to travel throughout the country managing the firm's business, an experience which provided him with vital insights into the Russian peasant mentality and way of life. Three years later, however, the firm foundered, and Leskov began a career as a journalist, first in Kiev and later in St Petersburg. He became involved in St Petersburg politics, but was unable to find a comfortable stance amid the deep split between conservatives and radicals and was viewed as an outsider by both camps. Leskov's first published fiction, *The Musk Ox* (1863), reflected his difficult years in St Petersburg, and the inability of idealistic urban radicals to identify with the reality of peasant life.

In 1864, two years after separating from Vasilevna, Leskov met Katerina Bubnova, who was to give him a third child, Andrei. The following year, he produced his best-known work, *Lady Macbeth of Mtsensk*; a story too shocking and dispassionate to be fully appreciated by its nineteenth-century audience, it inspired an equally controversial opera by Shostakovich. Leskov wrote copiously during the latter part of the nineteenth century, but often failed to find a secure readership. He did, however, have a few notable successes, including *The Sealed Angel* (1873), whose popularity in high places enabled him to secure a position in the Ministry of Education.

In 1875, frustrated at the literary and political world's dismissal of him, and experiencing problems in his unofficial marriage, Leskov left Russia for a visit to Paris. Here he experienced something of a spiritual crisis, which began to turn him against the Orthodox Church. He started to develop a form of spiritual Christianity, similar to that of Tolstoy, whom he greatly admired, and separated from Bubnova in an attempt to live as a celibate. His criticism of the Orthodox Church brought him yet more controversy and rejection, and towards the end of his life Leskov grew increasingly embittered, both at his treatment and at the moral underdevelopment of the people of Russia. He died of angina in 1895.

Robert Chandler's poems have appears in the *Times Literary Supplement* and *Poetry Review*. His translations of Sappho and Apollinaire have been published in the *Everyman's Poetry* series, and he has been a regular contributor for many years to the journal *Modern Poetry in Translation*. He is the translator of Vasily Grossman's 'Life and Fate', and the co-translator of five volumes of the work of Andrey Platonov. He has also translated Pushkin's *Dubrovsky* for Hesperus Press.

HESPERUS PRESS – 100 PAGES

Hesperus Press, as suggested by the Latin motto, is committed to bringing near what is far – far both in space and time. Works written by the greatest authors, and unjustly neglected or simply little known in the English-speaking world, are made accessible through new translations and a completely fresh editorial approach. Through these short classic works, each around 100 pages in length, the reader will be introduced to the greatest writers from all times and all cultures.

For more information on Hesperus Press, please visit our website: **www.hesperuspress.com**

ET REMOTISSIMA PROPE

SELECTED TITLES FROM HESPERUS PRESS

Author	Title	Foreword writer
Pietro Aretino	*The School of Whoredom*	Paul Bailey
Jane Austen	*Love and Friendship*	Fay Weldon
Honoré de Balzac	*Colonel Chabert*	A.N. Wilson
Charles Baudelaire	*On Wine and Hashish*	Margaret Drabble
Giovanni Boccaccio	*Life of Dante*	A.N. Wilson
Charlotte Brontë	*The Green Dwarf*	Libby Purves
Mikhail Bulgakov	*The Fatal Eggs*	Doris Lessing
Giacomo Casanova	*The Duel*	Tim Parks
Miguel de Cervantes	*The Dialogue of the Dogs*	
Anton Chekhov	*The Story of a Nobody*	Louis de Bernières
Wilkie Collins	*Who Killed Zebedee?*	Martin Jarvis
Arthur Conan Doyle	*The Tragedy of the Korosko*	Tony Robinson
William Congreve	*Incognita*	Peter Ackroyd
Joseph Conrad	*Heart of Darkness*	A.N. Wilson
Gabriele D'Annunzio	*The Book of the Virgins*	Tim Parks
Dante Alighieri	*New Life*	Louis de Bernières
Daniel Defoe	*The King of Pirates*	Peter Ackroyd
Marquis de Sade	*Incest*	Janet Street-Porter
Charles Dickens	*The Haunted House*	Peter Ackroyd
Fyodor Dostoevsky	*Poor People*	Charlotte Hobson
Joseph von Eichendorff	*Life of a Good-for-nothing*	
George Eliot	*Amos Barton*	Matthew Sweet
F. Scott Fitzgerald	*The Rich Boy*	John Updike
Gustave Flaubert	*Memoirs of a Madman*	Germaine Greer
E.M. Forster	*Arctic Summer*	Anita Desai
Ugo Foscolo	*Last Letters of Jacopo Ortis*	Valerio Massimo Manfredi
Elizabeth Gaskell	*Lois the Witch*	Jenny Uglow

Théophile Gautier	*The Jinx*	Gilbert Adair
André Gide	*Theseus*	
Nikolai Gogol	*The Squabble*	Patrick McCabe
Thomas Hardy	*Fellow-Townsmen*	Emma Tennant
Nathaniel Hawthorne	*Rappaccini's Daughter*	Simon Schama
E.T.A. Hoffmann	*Mademoiselle de Scudéri*	Gilbert Adair
Victor Hugo	*The Last Day of a Condemned Man*	Libby Purves
Joris-Karl Huysmans	*With the Flow*	Simon Callow
Henry James	*In the Cage*	Libby Purves
Franz Kafka	*Metamorphosis*	Martin Jarvis
Heinrich von Kleist	*The Marquise of O–*	Andrew Miller
D.H. Lawrence	*The Fox*	Doris Lessing
Leonardo da Vinci	*Prophecies*	Eraldo Affinati
Giacomo Leopardi	*Thoughts*	Edoardo Albinati
Niccolò Machiavelli	*Life of Castruccio Castracani*	Richard Overy
Katherine Mansfield	*In a German Pension*	Linda Grant
Guy de Maupassant	*Butterball*	Germaine Greer
Herman Melville	*The Enchanted Isles*	Margaret Drabble
Francis Petrarch	*My Secret Book*	Germaine Greer
Luigi Pirandello	*Loveless Love*	
Edgar Allan Poe	*Eureka*	Sir Patrick Moore
Alexander Pope	*Scriblerus*	Peter Ackroyd
Alexander Pushkin	*Dubrovsky*	Patrick Neate
François Rabelais	*Gargantua*	Paul Bailey
François Rabelais	*Pantagruel*	Paul Bailey
Friedrich von Schiller	*The Ghost-seer*	Martin Jarvis
Percy Bysshe Shelley	*Zastrozzi*	Germaine Greer
Stendhal	*Memoirs of an Egotist*	Doris Lessing